Take a deep breath, tur...
faced with an enemy par...
struggling to control a tir...
storm; Amita and Jonath...
department store destroyed by a terrorist bomb; and many other
courageous young people involved in daring exploits and

AMAZING ADVENTURE STORIES

COLLECTED BY
TONY BRADMAN

Illustrated by Jon Riley

CORGI BOOKS

AMAZING ADVENTURE STORIES
A CORGI BOOK : 0 552 52768 8

First published in Great Britain by Doubleday,
a division of Transworld Publishers Ltd

PRINTING HISTORY
Doubleday edition published 1994
Corgi edition published 1995
Corgi edition reprinted 1996

Corgi Books are published by Transworld Publishers Ltd,
61–63 Uxbridge Road, London W5 5SA,
in Australia by Transworld Publishers (Australia) Pty Ltd,
15–25 Helles Avenue, Moorebank, NSW 2170
and in New Zealand by Transworld Publishers (NZ) Ltd,
3 William Pickering Drive, Albany, Auckland.

Printed and bound in Great Britain by
Cox & Wyman Ltd, Reading, Berkshire.

CONTENTS

DADDY-LONG-LEGS
by Robert Westall

Granda's house was much too close to Hitler.

The only people in Garmouth who lived closer than us were the lighthouse-keepers on the end of the piers. All there was between us and Hitler was the North Sea. On sunny evenings I used to watch the little white fat clouds blowing eastward, and think that by morning they would be looking down on places in Norway and Denmark and Holland where grey soldiers strutted around doing the goose-step in their jackboots, and people crept about in fear of a hand on their shoulder. I even worried about the clouds a bit.

We were on a tiny headland that jutted out into the mouth of the Tyne. Not worth defending, the soldiers from the Castle said, as they laid their long

1

corkscrews of barbed wire inland from us. There was a checkpoint a hundred yards away up the pier road, where sometimes, with bayonets fixed to the rifles on their shoulders, they demanded to see our identity cards. But usually they let us through with a wink and a thumbs-up, because they knew us.

The Old Coastguard House, they called my grandfather's house. It was really only a white-painted cottage, with a little tower one storey higher than the roof. The tower had great windows, watching the Tyne on the right, the bay of Prior's Haven on the left, and the Castle beyond, and the North Sea in front. My granda had stuck great criss-crosses of sticky tape over the windows, to save us being cut to bits by flying glass if a bomb fell near. He had scrounged a lot of sandbags from the soldiers, in exchange for the odd bottle of my grandmother's elderberry wine. The soldiers were very keen on my grandmother's elderberry. They said a nip of it was as good as a tot of whisky when you were freezing on guard-duty of a winter's night. My granda filled the sandbags with soil from the garden, leaving a great hole which filled with water when it rained in winter. My grandfather considered keeping ducks on it, but he thought the firing of the Castle guns would scare them witless during air-raids, and besides, the pond dried out completely in summer. A pity, because the ducks' eggs would have helped the war effort.

My grandfather built up the sandbags round
the windows of the cottage, till we looked a real
fortress. Of course he couldn't sandbag the tower
windows, they were too high up. But nobody was
supposed to go up there during air-raids.

I think people worried about us, stuck out there
on our little headland. They offered us an Anderson
air-raid shelter for the garden; but Granda said he
preferred our cellar, which had walls three feet
thick. They offered to evacuate us altogether. But
Granda said he wasn't going to run away from
Hitler, into some council house. He would face
Hitler where he stood; and he ran up the Union
Jack on our flagpole every morning to prove it. He
and I did it together, standing to attention, then
we saluted the flag and Granda said, 'God save the
King,' without fail. Grandma said we should take
it down during air-raids, as it would make us a
target. Granda just made a noise of contempt, deep
in his throat. Otherwise, though, Grandma was as
keen on the war effort as we were, collecting in the
National Savings every Tuesday morning, knitting
comforts for the troops, keeping eggs fresh in Isin-
glass, and bottling all the fruit she could lay her
hands on.

I remember I'd just got home from school that
December night. The cottage looked dark and lonely, and my guts scrunched up a bit, as they always
did when I passed the checkpoint and said ta-ta to

the soldiers, who always called me 'Sunny Jim'. Granda would still be at work down the fish quay, and Grandma would be finishing her shopping up in Shields. There would be a lot to do: the blackout curtains to draw, the lamps to light (for we had no electricity) and the ready-laid fire to set a match to. Grandma had left some old potatoes in a bowl of water, which meant she wanted me to peel them for supper and put the peelings in the swill-bucket for Mason's pig . . .

I had just lit the last lamp, in the kitchen, and was rolling up my sleeves to tackle the potatoes, when I saw the daddy-long-legs come cruising across the room. It was a big one, a whopper. It looked nearly as big as a German bomber, and I hated it as much. I mean, I love bees and ladybirds, but daddy-long-legs hang about you and suddenly scrape against your bare skin with their scratchy, traily legs. Given half a chance they get down the back of your neck. It was long past the season for them, but this one must have been hibernating or something, and been awakened by a sudden warmth. I backed off, and grabbed an old copy of Granda's *Daily Express* and prepared to swat it. But it had no interest in me. It made straight for the oil-lamp, and banged against the glass shade with that awful persistent pinging. And then suddenly it went down inside, between the shade and the glass chimney. I could still hear it pinging and see

4

its shadow, magnified on the frosted glass. God, it must be getting pretty hot down there . . .

I squinted down cautiously between the shade and the hot chimney. It was hurling itself against the chimney, mad to reach the flame. Silly thing, it would do itself an injury . . . Then I noticed that one of its long crooked legs had already fallen off. As I watched, another broke off. But still the creature hurled itself against the chimney. Another leg went, then another, and there was a stink of burning that was not paraffin. Then it fell against the chimney with a sharp sizzle and lay still at last, just a little dirty mark. There was a tiny wisp of smoke; the stink was awful.

Feeling a bit sick, because it had been a living thing, I went back to peeling the potatoes.

It was then that the siren went. I ran to the door, slipped through the blackout curtain and went outside to look for Granda and Grandma. It was quite dark by that time; but I heard a distant tiny fizz, and the first searchlight came on at the Castle. A dim, poor yellow beam at first, but quickly followed by a brilliant white beam, so bright it looked nearly solid. High up, little wisps of cloud trailed through the beam, like cigarette smoke. Then another beam and another. Four, five, six, all swinging out to seawards, groping for Jerry like the fingers of a robot's hand. Then more, dimmer, searchlights, up towards Blyth. And more still, across the river in South Shields. It made me proud; we were ready for them, waiting.

But in the deep blue reflected light, which lit up the pier road like moonlight, there was no sign of Granda or Grandma. I could see the two sentries on the checkpoint, huddling behind their sandbags, the ends of their fags like little red pin-points. They'd be in trouble for that, if this raid was more than a false alarm. You can see a fag-end from five thousand feet up, my Granda says . . .

But otherwise, the pier road was empty. And there was no chance of them coming now; the wardens would force them down some shelter, until the raid was over. I was on my own. I felt a silly impulse to run up and join the sentries, but they'd only send me back into cover. And besides, it was time to be brave. I checked the stirrup-pump with its red buckets of water, in case they dropped incendiaries. Then I did what I was supposed to do, and went down the cellar to shelter.

But there was nothing to do down there. By the light of the oil-lamp, trembling slightly in my hand because it was so heavy, all I could see was Granda's three sacks of spare potatoes, and the dusty rows of Grandma's bottles of elderberry. This year's still had little Christmas balloons, yellow, red and blue, fastened over their necks. They were still fermenting. Some of the balloons were small but fat and shiny; others looked all shrivelled and shrunken.

I should sit down on a mattress and be good. But it was cold and I couldn't hear anything. I mean, the Jerries might be overhead; they might have dropped incendiaries by this time, the cottage roof might be burning, and how would I know? When he was there, in an air-raid, Granda kept nipping upstairs for a look-see. As the person in charge of the cottage tonight, so should I. Or so I told myself.

I crept upstairs. Nothing was on fire. Everything was silent, except for some frantic dog barking on and on, up the town.

And then I heard it; very faint, far out over the sea. *Vroomah, vroomah, vroomah.* Jerry was coming. You could always tell Jerry, because the Raff planes made a steady drone. But Jerry's engines weren't synchronized, Granda said.

And as I went on listening, I knew there was more than one of them. The whole sea was full of their echoes. My stomach drew itself up like a fist. I wasn't scared; just ready. Your stomach always does that.

Then the whole blue scene turned bright pale yellow. The earth shook, and the universe seemed to crack apart like an egg. The Castle guns had fired. I waited, counting under my breath. Seventeen, eighteen, nineteen. Four brilliant stars out to sea burnt black holes in my eyes. They were in a

7

W-shape, and everywhere I looked now there were four black dots in a W-shape. Then the sound of explosions, rolling in across the water like waves. Then the echoes going away down the coast, off every cliff, fainter and fainter.

The guns fired again. People were rude about those guns. They said they never hit anything; that they couldn't hit a barn-door at ten yards. That the gunners should get their eyes checked. But, tonight . . . There was suddenly a light out to sea, high in the air. A little yellow light where no light should be. The Jerries never showed a light, any more than we did.

But this light grew. And now it was falling, falling. Like a shooting star, when we say that it is the soul of someone dying.

And I knew what it was. We'd hit one. It was going to crash. I leapt up and down in tremendous glee.

Burn, Jerry, burn. We'd had too many folk killed in raids for us to love the Jerries any more.

It never reached the sea. There was such a flash as made the guns look like a piddling Guy Fawkes' night and a bang that hurt my ears. But I could still hear faint cheering – from the Castle, from across the river; very faint, in South Shields. Then there was just a shower of red fragments, falling to the water.

But the rest of the planes came on. The guns went

on firing. They were nearly overhead now. There was a faint whispering in the air, then a rattle on the pantiles of Granda's house above me. I ducked down into the cellar entrance. It seemed especially silly to be killed by falling *British* shrapnel . . .

I didn't poke my head out again until it was quiet. Far up the river, the bangs were still lighting up the sky. The red lines of pom-pom tracers climbed so slowly, so lazily. Then the whooshing flicker of the Home Guard's rocket-batteries. And the tremor of the first bombs coming, through the soles of my shoes. It was Newcastle that was copping it tonight . . . we could do with a break.

It was so peaceful, to seawards. Just the faint blue light from the searchlights, which could have been moonlight . . .

And then, by that light, I saw it. White, like a slowly drifting mushroom.

A Jerry parachute. I could see the little black dot of the man, under his harness. He was going to land in the water of the harbour; he was going to get very wet, and that would cool his courage, as Grandma always said. He might drown . . .

The parachute collapsed slowly into the water about two or three hundred yards out. Ah well, they'd pick him up. The picket-boat on the defence-boom that lay right across the river. It would be full of armed sailors. I was just an interested spectator.

But for some reason, the picket-boat continued

to stay moored to the far end of the boom. There was no sound from its heavy diesel engine. Come on, come on! The bloke might drown . . . Or he might come ashore and do anything. Myself, I hoped he drowned.

But I watched and watched, and that boat never stirred. Maybe they hadn't noticed the parachute; maybe they'd been following the raid up the river, like I'd just been doing . . . Maybe the Jerry wasn't drowning; maybe he was swimming ashore at this very moment.

And we were the nearest bit of shore.

I decided to run for the sentries. But at that moment, a second wave of bombers droned in. The shellbursts overhead were churning the sky into a deafening porridge of flashes. I could hear the shrapnel falling, rattling on the roof again. I daren't go out. I'd seen what shrapnel had done to one of Grandpa's rabbits, old Chinnie. I had found her. The roof of her hutch was smashed in, and the floor, and Chinnie lay like a bloody cushion, blue Chinchilla fur hammered into the ground in a mass of wooden splinters and fluff . . .

I hovered piteously from foot to foot. Oh, please God, send him to land somewhere else. South Shields, the rocks below the Castle . . .

I thought at first it was a seal in the water. We get the odd seal up the Gar; they come in for the guts from the fish-gutting, when they're really hungry – even though the Gar is an oily, stinking old river. Sometimes they bob around out there and stare at the land, the water shining on their sleek dark heads.

But seals don't have a pale white blob where their face should be. And seals don't rise up out of the water till their shoulders are showing, then their whole bodies, the gap between their legs. They don't haul themselves out of the water and begin to climb the low soily cliff.

Oh, God, let the guns stop, let the shrapnel stop! But a third wave was vrooming in overhead, and a piece of shrapnel suddenly smashed our front gate into a shower of white fragments.

Suddenly, I made up my mind that I would rather be smashed to a bloody pulp by British shrapnel than be in the power of the Swastika. Holding my arms above my head in an absolutely hopeless attempt to protect myself, I ran for the smashed gate.

As I went through it, a very big, very strong hand grabbed me. I think I squealed like a shot rabbit my father had once had to kill with a blow to the back of the neck. I think I kicked out and bucked wildly, just like that very rabbit, fighting for its life. My efforts were equally useless. The huge hand carried me back to the front door and flung me inside. Our little hall was filled with a huge gasping and panting. Our front door slammed

11

shut. The hand picked me up again and carried me into the living-room and threw me on a couch. And for the first time, I saw him.

He was huge, black, shining and dripping water all over Grandma's carpet. He trailed tentacles from his body with little shining metal bits on the end. And he did look like a seal, with the leather helmet almost crushing his head in so that only his eyes showed, and his pale long nose, and his mouth, gaping like a fish's.

'Others?' he shouted. 'Others?' He stared around him wildly, then seemed to remember something suddenly and felt, groped at, his shining, dripping side. And pulled out something black with a long tube . . .

I recognized it from the war magazine that my father used to buy me, before he joined the Raff. It was a Luger automatic pistol, with a twelve-shot magazine. All the Jerry aircrew carried them.

He tore off his leather helmet as if it suddenly hurt him. It made him look a bit more human; he had fair hair, quite long, a bit like our Raff types, which surprised me. Funny how you can still be surprised, even when you're almost wetting your-self with terror . . .

'Others?' he said a third time. He was listening. It made him look like a wild animal, alert. Then I twigged what he was getting at. Was anybody else in the house? Then he grabbed me again, shouting,

'*Raus, Raus!*' and dragged me from room to room by my hair.

When we had searched everywhere, even the lookout tower and the cellar, he brought me back and threw me on the couch again. He listened to the outside; the raid had quietened. But he was still shaking. Then he fell into Granda's chair, and we stared at each other. I didn't much like the look of him at all. He had green eyes, too close together. My Granda always says never to trust a man who has eyes too close together.

Then he pointed the gun at me (I think he enjoyed pointing the gun at me) and said, 'Food!'

What could I do but lead him to Grandma's larder? And get him our only half-loaf from the enamel bread-bin. And the butter-dish from the top shelf, with our tiny ration of butter and marge, mixed together so it would last longer. I began to cut a thin slice, but he pushed me aside into a corner with the gun-barrel, then put the gun down and smeared the whole half-loaf with all the butter and marge and began to wolf it down, tearing off huge chunks. I noticed he had very large white teeth, a bit like tombstones. When he had gulped it all down, he poked me into the larder with the gun again, and went along the shelves to see what else he could find. He found our little cheese-ration and swallowed it in one mouthful, just tearing off

14

the greaseproof paper with his large teeth, and swallowing so fast you could tell from the gulp he gave that it hurt him. He found a quarter-jar of jam and began to eat it with a spoon, his gun in his left hand now. Then three shrivelled apples, which he stuffed into a pocket of his dripping suit. Didn't they feed them, before they came on a raid? Were all the Germans starving, like our propaganda used to say, back in the Phoney War?

How did I feel? I felt the end of the world had come, the worst had happened. That I, alone, in Garmouth, was already under the Nazi jackboot. That I was now already inside the Third Reich. He might do anything to me . . .

And yet nothing was changed; the fire still burned on steadily, making steam rise from his suit, as he sat by it. There were Granda's old pipes in their rack, and a twist of tobacco in its silver paper. There was Grandma's knitting still in her chair. The world had turned insane.

And then I began to worry about Granda and Gran. Soon, the raid would be over. Soon they would come walking down the pier road, and straight into . . . Granda might try and do something; he was as brave as a lion. The German would shoot him. Then he might shoot Gran too . . . But what could I do? Nothing. Even when the noise of the raid stopped, there was no point in shouting.

The sentries on the checkpoint would never hear me. And then he would shoot *me* . . .

He was watching me now.

'Derink!' he said. 'Derink. Derink!' He made a drinking motion with his free hand.

Like a slave, I crept into the kitchen. A slave of the Third Reich. I got our half-bottle of milk from the cooler on the floor, put it on the kitchen table, and turned to get the tea and sugar canisters and the teapot . . .

'Derink!' he shouted again, and swept them all off on to the floor in his rage. The milk bottle broke and the milk and fragments went everywhere. 'Derink!' He raised his hand to his lips again, and threw his head back. I could tell from the shape his fingers made, that he meant he wanted a bottle. He pointed down the cellar. '*Wein . . . vin . . . wine!*'

He must have noticed the row of bottles, Gran's elderberry, when he searched the cellar. I took up the oil-lamp and went down for some. He didn't follow me; only stood by the cellar door, listening to the outside.

The long rows of bottles glistened in the lamplight. They were arranged by year. Gran kept her elderberry a long time . . .

And then it came to me. Gran's elderberry . . . people laughed at it because it wasn't proper wine.

But it was strong stuff. She gave the curate from the church a glass of her old batch once, and he liked it so much he'd accepted a second . . .

He was so drunk by the time he reached Front Street that he fell off his bicycle. Elderberry gets stronger every year you keep it. This year's – 1940 – still fermenting, wouldn't do him any harm. But 1939 . . . 1938 . . . I picked up two bottles of her 1938, dusted them with my hand, and carried them upstairs.

He gave a quick, wolfish grin. *'Wein? Ja! Ja!'* He couldn't get a bottle open quick enough. Pulled the cork out with his strong tombstone teeth and spat it out, so it bounced on the hearth-rug. Then he raised the bottle, threw back his head and the sound of glugging filled the room. It was already much more than the curate ever had.

He stopped at last to draw breath. His wolfish grin was wider.

'Wein. Ja. Gut!' He seemed to relax as it hit him. Stretched his legs out to the fire. Then he had a long think and said, quite clearly but slowly, *'Engländer* not our natural enemy are!' He seemed quite pleased with himself. Then he took another swig and announced, *'Engländer* little *Brüders* . . . broth . . . brothers are.' He put down the bottle for a moment, and reached out and patted me on the shoulder. Then he picked up the bottle

again and offered it to me, indicating that I drink too.

I made a right mess of it. I didn't want to drink, get drunk, and yet I had to. Otherwise he might suspect I was trying to poison him . . .

So I drank, and it went down the wrong way, and I sprayed it all over the place and went into a helpless fit of coughing.

He threw back his head and laughed as if he thought that was hilarious.

'*Wein* . . . not . . . little *Brüders ist*. Big men . . . *Wein*.' He drank some more. The bottle was half-empty by now. The more he got, the more he seemed to want. And, oddly, the better it made his English.

'English little *Brüders* . . . but Europe is corrupt . . . we must make a new order . . . then . . . happy!'

I just waited patiently. Time was on my side now.

It began to have an effect on him. He began to slump deeper into his chair. But the hand with the gun kept playing with it twitchily. I was dead scared it might go off. And he wasn't grinning any more. He looked at me solemnly, owlishly.

'*Prost* . . . drink toast. To Rudi! *Mein Kamerad!*' More wine glugged down, while I waited. Then he said, in a small hopeless voice, 'Rudi *ist tot* . . . dead. *Und* Karli, *und* Maxi, *und* Heini. *Alles* . . . *tot*.'

And then, unbelieving, I saw a tear run down his face. Then another and another. He put his face in his hands and sobbed like a woman, only worse, because women know how to cry properly. He was just a gulping, sniffing, revolting mess. I reckoned that any minute I'd be able to snatch the gun from where it lay. But I didn't know how to use it . . .

'*Kamerad*, *Kamerad*,' he moaned; comrades, comrades. He was rocking in his chair, like a woman rocking a baby.

And I just waited. Then he began to sing, like a lot of drunks do. Something about '*Ich habe einen Kamerad*'. It was horrible. It embarrassed me so much my toes squirmed inside my shoes.

But I went on waiting.

Finally he stopped, a stupid look of alarm growing on his face. He tried to get up and failed, falling back heavily into the chair. He tried again, pressing down with his hands on the chair-arms. And since he had the bottle in one hand, and the gun in the other, he didn't make it again. The hand holding the bottle opened, and the bottle fell to the rug with a dull clunk and rolled towards me, spilling out a trail of dark elderberry.

Slowly, at last, like a very old man, he managed to lever himself to his feet, and stood swaying above me. I thought he was going to shoot me then. But he decided not to; perhaps he remembered he had sent me for the wine – his little slave-labourer.

Instead, he made a wavering track for the door, crashing into every bit of furniture on the way, hurting himself and gasping. Suddenly he reminded me of something. And I remembered what it was. The daddy-long-legs, in the oil lamp. Like it, he had come flying in; like it, he was dashing himself to bits. I almost laughed out loud. Except that pistol was wavering all over the room.

Then it suddenly went off. Even in the middle of that raid, the noise was deafening. A panel of the door suddenly wasn't there, and the air was full of a Guy Fawkes smell, and the smell of splintered wood. That piney, resinous smell.

Then the gun went off again. He cried out, and I saw blood pouring from a tear in the leg of his wetsuit. And then, with a wild yell, he was out of the front door and the wind was blowing in.

I think I ran across to, of all things, replace the blackout curtain. We were trained so hard to keep the blackout; it was second nature. But as soon as my hand was on it, I heard a yell and a big splash from outside. I knew what had happened. He had fallen into our sandbag-hole – the hole we had thought of using for a duck-pond.

I ran to see. He was just a series of sodden humps, face-down in the water. He didn't move at all. Suddenly a mass of bubbles rose and burst where his face would be, under the water. It was unbelievable. I mean, that hole was only about seven feet across. There wasn't a foot of water in it.

And yet I knew he was drowning. As I watched, one hand came up out of the water and clawed at the side. But it couldn't get a grip, because the sides were steep and slippery. His head turned, his face looked at me and then fell back, and more bubbles came from his mouth.

Soon, any minute now, he would move for the last time; then he would be dead. One dead murderer; one dead Nazi thug.

What made me jump into the hole beside him? Try to lift him out and fail, for he was far too heavy for my eleven years? What made me force my legs under his head and lift his face clear of the filthy, muddy water, so that he could groan and choke and breathe and mutter to himself in a language I would never understand. '*Freund, Freund*!' His big hand wandered round my body, till I grabbed it and held on to it.

'*Freund, Freund.*'

And that was how we stayed, while the returning bombers droned back over us, and the guns fired intermittently, and the shrapnel sang its awful song to earth.

And that was how Granda and Gran found us, and stared at my mud-stained face, after the all-clear had gone. By the light of the fires from the burning docks at Newcastle.

'God love the bairn,' said my gran. 'What's he doin' wi' that feller?'

Granda took a careful look. 'Reckon that feller's a Jerry. Run for the sentries up at the wire, Martha.'

I had nothing to say. I was so cold I could not move my jaws any more. But I kept wondering why I did what I did. He was a murderer. Maybe he was the pilot who dropped the bomb that killed my mother at Newcastle, when she'd just nipped down to the shops for a box of matches to light our fire.

That's when my dad joined the Raff. To get revenge.

So why couldn't I just let him lie there and die? I thought a lot about that. It wasn't because he'd ever been nice or likeable; it wasn't even because he'd cried for his dead mates. It wasn't even because if I'd let him die, *I* would have killed him. It was a heroic thing to kill a Nazi in those days. Everyone would have thought me a hero.

No, it was just that he was still alive. And I didn't want him dead in Granda's garden. I mean, if he'd died, he'd still be there, to me. Even if Granda filled the duck-pond in; which he did, a few days later, shovelling soil from all over the garden into it, furiously. Saying it was a danger in the blackout.

His name was Konrad Huess. I know because he wrote to me after the war, to thank me. Sent me lots of photos of his wife and kids. I was glad, then. For his wife and kids. But I never replied. I was too mixed-up.

I still am.

HOSTAGE
by Malorie Blackman

When I left school after my detention, it was already beginning to get dark. Zipping up my anorak right to my chin, I wondered what to do next. I wasn't going back to our house, that was for sure. Kicking through the snow surrounding my wellies, I decided to go to the precinct. Yeah! A trip to the precinct for an ice-cream and then maybe the cinema meant that I could put off seeing Dad. I didn't want to see him at all – not after the blazing row we'd had that morning before I left for school.

I hated our house – I never called it home. Now that Mum had gone, it was always so lonely, so desperately quiet. Even when Dad and I were together, we never seemed to have much to say to each other.

I dug into my pockets. A couple of safety pins,

a cracked mirror, chewing gum, an unused plaster, my comb, the end of a pencil, my front door keys – but not much money. So much for the cinema! Just an ice-cream then.

'Angela? Angela Henshaw?'

At the sound of my name, I turned my head. A woman with dark brown hair tied back in a pony-tail smiled at me from behind the wheel of a dark-coloured Rover. I was sure I'd never seen her before, so how did she know my name? Her car crawled along at a snail's pace as she kept up with me. I stopped walking. She stopped the car, although the engine was still running.

'Angela Henshaw?' she said again.

'Yeah?' I replied suspiciously, backing away from her.

From nowhere, a warm, rough hand that smelt of paraffin clamped over my mouth and an arm braced around my waist like a vice. Before I could even blink, I was lifted off my feet. Somewhere above and behind me I could hear a man's voice, but I couldn't make out what he was saying over the sound of my heart slamming against my ribs. By the time I thought to struggle and kick, I'd been bundled into the car and, with a screech of brakes, it went tearing down the road.

It all happened so quickly.

I looked around, my head jerking like a puppet's. A blond man in a light grey raincoat sat on my right; a bald man in a navy-blue leather jacket sat on my left. I was jammed between them so tightly, I felt like toothpaste being squeezed out of a tube.

Terrified, I opened my mouth and *screamed*. Just as loud as I could. But I only got out about three seconds' worth before the bald man clamped his hand over my mouth.

'Shut up! SHUT UP!' he hissed at me.

His breath reeked of garlic. From the smell of his hand, he was the same man who'd grabbed me off the pavement. I tried to scream through his fingers but the air rushed back into my throat, making me cough.

'Listen to me,' said Baldy. 'We're not going to hurt you. We just want to make sure that your dad does what we want. As soon as he does, we'll let you go and tell him where to pick you up. D'you understand?'

I didn't answer. I *couldn't* answer. The way my stomach was churning, if I opened my mouth I'd be sick all over my trousers.

'Don't scream again, not unless you want to seriously cheese me off,' said the other man, the blond, his ice-blue eyes giving me frostbite. Baldy began to slowly remove his fingers from over my mouth. I opened my mouth to scream again. I didn't even get out one second's worth this time. Baldy's fingers were back over my mouth.

'Right. If that's the way you want it,' he said, glaring at me.

His hand over my mouth was pressing down so hard, it hurt. His thick fingers covered almost all of my nostrils as well as my mouth. I couldn't breathe. My lungs were going to burst. I tried pulling at his fingers with both of my hands but he just clamped down harder. I looked up at him, my eyes stinging with tears. He frowned down at me, then relaxed his grip slightly. I tilted my head back, dragging air down into my lungs. I wanted to scream and shout and throw myself at the car doors. I had a tight feeling in my stomach and a tighter feeling in my chest.

Don't panic . . . keep calm . . . think . . . The words filled my head as I tried – unsuccessfully – to stop myself from shaking like a leaf. I forced myself to take one deep breath, then another and another.

What should I do?

'That's better, Angela,' said Baldy softly. 'Just do as we say and we'll all be better off.'

'Literally!' laughed the blond man. A smug, vicious laugh that sent an icy chill trickling down my spine.

I looked out of the windows, ready to launch myself at one of the car doors to attract someone's attention the moment an opportunity arose, but the driver obviously knew Deansea very well. She kept to the back streets where there were very few people and no traffic lights around.

What should I do?

Baldy had spoken of Dad doing something they wanted. Was that why they'd grabbed me? It had to be. Dad was the manager of the best jewellery shop in our small town. I'd always reckoned that Dad chose the jewellery shop when he left the army, because it was one of the few shops in Deansea where he wouldn't be bothered with children day in, day out. Dad never did like children. Not even me.

The car jolted, bringing me back to the present and my predicament. My heart was still hammering, hammering, and there was the strangest taste in my mouth. Several moments passed before I realized just what the strange taste might be. *Fear.*

We finally left Deansea by the old Church Road.

'Blindfold her!' the woman commanded.

The blond man retrieved what looked like a ladies scarf from behind him. It was covered in purple and red and burgundy swirls.

'Do we really have to do that?' frowned Baldy. 'We'll be long gone before they find her. What does it matter if she sees where we're going?'

The woman glanced around to glare at him. Then she turned to the other man. 'Do as I say,' she ordered, before turning back to the road.

'No! NO!' I screamed.

I couldn't help it. I freaked. No way was I going to let them blindfold me without even putting up a fight. I kicked and hit out at the blond man as hard as I could. Baldy grabbed me by the arms and tried to pull me away from his friend. The blond man tried to get the blindfold over my eyes anyway, so the moment one of his hands came within range I bit down – *hard*. He swore fluently, then grabbed me away from Baldy and shook me over and over again.

'Do that one more time and I'll make sure your dad never sees you again. At least, not in one piece. D'you understand?' he hissed.

I didn't answer.

'D'YOU UNDERSTAND?' he shouted.

I nodded, terrified.

'Good. Now keep still,' he said.

I couldn't have moved then, even if my life depended on it. I remembered how just a few minutes ago – or was it hours? – I'd not wanted to go home because I didn't want to see Dad. Now I wondered if I'd ever see him again.

They had to be after Dad's jewels. There was no other explanation. But there was one big question. Would Dad really hand over all his precious jewels just for me? After our blazing row that morning, I really doubted it. And it wasn't just this morning.

It seemed like ever since Mum left, Dad and I had done nothing *but* quarrel.

I'm not beaten yet, not by any means, I thought desperately.

I leaned back against the seat, feeling the double knot used to secure the blindfold digging into the back of my head.

'Don't panic,' I mouthed silently. 'Don't panic and stay alert.'

But it was so hard, when all I wanted to do was cry and never stop. My heart was still bouncing about in my chest and my stomach was turning over like a tumble-drier.

If you're going to be sick, do it over one of them – not over yourself, I thought.

The first thing to do was to get my bearings. I sat still between the two men and tried to think rationally. I tilted my head up slightly but I couldn't see under the blindfold. I lowered my head again. Now what?

Well . . . we'd left Deansea by the old Church Road, and since they'd blindfolded me, we'd been travelling for at least three minutes. How fast? Not as fast as my dad when he drove, so less than forty miles an hour? I couldn't be sure.

I started to count. When I'd reached six hundred, the car turned left. I started counting from one again – slow and steady, counting off the seconds. It was a trick Dad had been taught in the army. The only time we didn't seem to argue was when he was reminiscing about the army.

I carried on counting. The road wound around a bit but the car didn't slow down to make a proper turn until I reached one thousand four hundred, then it turned right. I counted to one hundred and twenty before the car turned right again. We must have turned on to a track or a field because the car – and everyone in it – bounced up and down as if we were all on a trampoline.

And all the time, no-one in the car said a word. I tried to memorize the route we were taking, like memorizing the numbers to open a safe. Six hundred left, fourteen hundred right, one hundred and twenty right. Abruptly the car stopped and the engine was turned off. I looked around as if to see through the scarf covering my eyes. I heard the driver's door open, followed by both the doors at the back. I sat still, listening to my kidnappers get out of the car.

'This way.'

My left arm was grabbed by Baldy and I was pulled out of the car. The snow was fresher here than in town. It crunched under my wellies. I heard the wind whistling in some tall trees to my right. We turned to the left and started walking. After ten steps the ground became firm as we entered some kind of house. I heard a door shut behind me. I'd never been so frightened by the sound of a door closing before.

After five steps, Baldy said gruffly, 'Stairs!'

I lifted my feet higher and started climbing up some steps. I counted twelve in all, the fifth one being the most creaky.

Suddenly I couldn't stop counting.

At the top of the stairs I was led into another room. I stood still.

'C–Can I t–take my blindfold off n–now?' I whispered, my hands moving up towards my eyes.

No–one tried to stop me so I pulled the blindfold off my face, blinking rapidly to focus. The room I was in was sombre, with blue painted walls and a wooden floor. Apart from the chair beside me, the only other piece of furniture was a table with a newspaper and a squashed lager can on it. Out of the corner of my eye I saw that the window had had planks of wood nailed across it. My kidnappers watched me. The silence in the room was deafening.

'W–What d'you want my dad to do?' I squeaked, more to hear myself speak than for any other reason, because I'd already guessed what they were after. But if I could speak then I was alive. And if I was alive, then I could get out of this. I *could*.

The two men regarded each other over my head.

'Let's just say, we want him to make a delivery,' said the blond.

'And he'd better not mess us about either,' said Baldy.

'A de–delivery . . .?' I stammered.

'Yeah!' Baldy grinned. 'One that . . .'

'Shut up, Quill!' the blond man snapped harshly.

'We're not supposed to use our names in front of the girl – remember?' the woman driver said quietly.

They all turned to look at me. I couldn't help it – I burst into tears.

What would Dad say if he could see me now . . .? In the past, whenever I felt like crying, I just had to think about what Dad would say if he caught me and the tears never got past my eyelids, but this time it didn't work. In fact, if anything, thinking of Dad just made me cry more.

If Dad was here instead of you, he wouldn't cry, I told myself. Nothing could ever make Dad cry.

'Tie her hands and legs together,' said the woman, after a long pause.

'I'll tie her to the chair,' said the blond man, moving forward.

'I'll do it,' said Quill.

'Don't you trust me?' snapped the blond man.

I kept my head down, still crying. As long as they were arguing amongst themselves, they wouldn't concentrate on me. The blond man was the one to be most wary of. All he cared about were the jewels from Dad's shop. I didn't matter. I was just a means to an end. And the woman was almost as bad. Only Quill thought of me as a person.

While crying, I wondered if I could or even should make a break for it. I could get past the two men, but the woman was right by the door. The woman walked over to Quill and whispered in his ear. I took a deep breath. It was now or never.

Quill moved forward to stand in front of me and the opportunity to make a break for it slipped away. Would I get another?

'When you've finished, come downstairs,' said the woman. 'I want to talk to you – *both* of you.'

The woman and the blond man left the room. I heard them walk downstairs. I turned to my captor.

'Don't tie me up, Quill,' I whispered. 'I couldn't bear it.'

'I've got no choice,' he said gruffly. 'And I'd forget that name if I were you. Don't use it in front of the others.'

I shook my head. I wasn't that stupid.

'Are you . . . after the jewels in Dad's shop? Is that the d–delivery you were all talking about?' I asked.

Quill took some thin, plastic rope out of his jacket pocket before nodding. My heart sunk to my toenails at the sight of it. Dad used the same kind for wrapping parcels at home. It was deceptively thin and very strong – almost unbreakable.

'Once we get the jewels, we'll let you go. I promise,' said Quill.

'And if Dad doesn't hand them over?'

'He wants you back, doesn't he?'

The question turned my blood cold – because that was the problem. *I didn't know*. Dad loved his shop and his jewels. When the quarrels between him and Mum became too bitter, when the atmosphere at home grew too tense, Dad always retreated to his shop. I'll never forget how Mum once sent me to fetch Dad from his 'precious hideout' (her words). When I arrived the shop was shut but I could see Dad through the window. For ages I watched him dust the displays of gold and silver necklaces, lovingly polish the gold rings, dust off the expensive gem stones. I actually felt jealous. Then I felt foolish and incredibly angry for being jealous of bits of metal and fancy glass. Still angry, I banged on the shop door so hard, I almost broke the glass. I remember how Dad had shouted at me for that too.

'Come on. This won't take long. Put your hands behind your back,' Quill ordered.

Slowly, reluctantly, I did as directed. Then I remembered something Dad had once told me –

something else he'd learnt in the army. Keeping my wrists together, I bent my hands back, with my palms as far apart from each other as I could get them. Quill tied my wrists together – tight. I sat down, then he squatted down to tie my ankles. I tried to keep my ankles together and my feet apart, flexing my feet upwards. Dad told me that if someone is tying you up, they'll need more rope to tie your hands and legs if you tense your muscles and flex your hands and feet. That way, when you relaxed, the ropes would be looser than if you simply relaxed to begin with. When Quill had finished he stood up.

'Do I have to gag you?' he asked.

I shook my head quickly. I couldn't bear the thought of something over my mouth.

'One single squeak out of you and I'll muzzle you like a dog. D'you understand?'

I nodded.

'There's no use shouting or screaming, we're miles from the nearest house. All you'll do is make the two downstairs very angry. D'you understand that?' Quill said.

I nodded again. I heard footsteps, then the other two came back into the room. The woman was carrying a cordless phone, the receiver to her ear.

'Mr Henshaw, you *will* do exactly as we say . . .' She stopped speaking.

I could hear Dad's furious voice at the other end of the line.

'Listen to me, Mr Henshaw,' the woman interrupted, her voice just as angry. 'I have someone here who'll persuade you to change your mind. Say hello to your father, Angela.'

She thrust the phone against my ear.

'Dad . . .' I whispered. 'Dad, is that you?'

'Angela . . .?' Dad was shocked. 'Angela, are you all right?' His voice was scared and angry, all at once.

'Dad, I'm frightened . . .' The receiver was yanked away from me.

'That's enough,' said the woman. She and the blond man left the room and started downstairs, all the time talking urgently into the phone.

'Like I said, behave yourself and you'll be home before you know it,' said Quill. And with that, he left the room, locking the door behind him. I sat perfectly still with my eyes closed, allowing the seconds to tick by. When I opened my eyes I was still tied up in a room I'd never seen before. I wasn't dreaming . . .

It was time to do something. I forced myself to relax. Immediately, my bonds felt looser. I stood up, my hands still behind my back. Then I lay down on the cold wooden floor, desperate not to make a sound. Lying on my side, I curled up tightly into a ball until I could slip my tied hands past my hips

38

and over the backs of my legs, slipping my feet, heels first, through the circle made by my arms. It took less than a minute – I'm very supple. Sitting up again, I worked away at the rope binding my feet.

The nylon rope cut into my fingers as I worked to unknot it, but at last it fell away from my ankles. Untying the rope that bound my hands was trickier. I had to use my teeth and the index finger of one hand and the thumb of the other to pry the knot open. But I did it.

Now what?

I stood up and silently moved over to the nailed-up window. That was no good. There was no way I could pull at the boards that covered the window without making some kind of noise that would alert my abductors.

'Don't just act. Think first,' I muttered.

Think . . . think . . . think . . . I looked in my pockets, hoping that something in there would give me an idea. I looked around. My mind was still a blank. I tiptoed across to the door. Even though I'd heard Quill turn the key in the lock, I turned the doorknob anyway. Nothing. But then, what did I expect? Putting my eye against the keyhole, I tried to see if one of my kidnappers was on the landing guarding my door, but I couldn't see a thing. The key was still in the lock from outside. I leant my head against the door, forcing my eyes wide open so I wouldn't cry again.

And that's when an idea sneaked into my head. A very dangerous idea . . .

I crept across the room to retrieve the newspaper. Laying it flat, I pushed it through the gap beneath the door, so that the newspaper was half on my side of the door, with the other half on the landing. I shuffled the newspaper so it was directly underneath the key. After putting a stick of chewing gum in my mouth, I straightened out one of the safety pins I had and started poking about in the lock. The key began to shift backwards until it dropped out of the lock, landing with a *clink* on the newspaper. I panicked. Had they heard it downstairs? Quickly I pulled the newspaper through to my side of the door. The door key was there on the newspaper. I froze, expecting to hear my kidnappers rush up the stairs at any moment.

Silence.

Unlocking the door, I opened it fully until it was almost touching the adjacent wall. I chewed harder on my chewing gum. Now came the hardest part of all. I ran over to the window and started banging my fists on the planks nailed across it.

'Help . . . HELP!' I screamed at the top of my lungs.

Immediately I heard footsteps thundering up the stairs.

Please let it be all of them . . . I prayed. I raced

across the room to stand behind the door. I wiped my sweaty hands on my coat, grasping the key to me.

'You were supposed to tie her up,' the woman said furiously.

'I did,' I heard Quill answer.

'The door's wide open,' said the blond man.

They all came racing into the room. This was it. I darted around the door and pulled it shut, jamming the key into the lock as I pulled it. My kidnappers shouted at me and I saw the blond man lunge at the door before it closed. Frantically, I turned the key in the lock. Only just in time. The doorknob rattled violently. Quickly taking the chewing gum out of my mouth, I stuffed it into the keyhole, using the end of the pencil I had to push it right in.

'Get out the way. I've got a spare key,' I heard the woman say.

For the first time since they'd captured me, I allowed myself a slight smile. I hadn't known for certain that they had a spare key. I'd just thought I'd better play safe. But now the woman's spare key wouldn't do her much good, not with the chewing gum and my pencil in the lock.

'Angela, open this door. NOW!' the blond man demanded.

Yeah! Likely! I thought, and raced down the stairs. I didn't have much time.

There it was – what I'd been looking for. *The telephone* . . .

The others were still shouting and screaming at me from upstairs. The doorknob rattled as they tried to open the door.

I picked up the receiver. Where would Dad be? At home or at his shop? I didn't have time to find out. It would be faster to phone the police. I dialled 999 and asked the emergency operator for the police. Upstairs, they were now trying to batter the door down. At last I was put through.

'Please help me. My name's Angela Henshaw. My dad owns Henshaw's Jewellers in the precinct. Listen! I've been kidnapped. The kidnappers left Deansea by the old Church Road. We drove for about three minutes straight, then six hundred left, fourteen hundred right, one hundred and twenty right. No! Don't interrupt! Ask Dad, he'll tell you what it means!' I rushed on urgently as the voice at the other end tried to cut in. 'I've been kidnapped and I don't know where . . .'

But at that moment, the upstairs door splintered. The noise crashed through the house. The next second lasted for ever. It was as if the very air in the house froze. I stood stricken in the hall.

Then everything happened at once. I heard shouting but I was too terrified to make out the words. And then came footsteps running – all over the sound of my heart thundering. I didn't wait to hear

any more. Almost blind with panic, I threw myself
at the front door. My hands were all thumbs as I
frantically pulled at the door latch.

Don't turn around . . . I kept telling myself that
over and over, as if by not turning around, I could
stop my kidnappers from catching me.

The door opened. It must have taken only a
second, two at the most, but that's not how it
felt.

'ANGELA . . .!'

'COME BACK HERE . . .'

From somewhere close behind me came the
voices of Baldy and the woman.

Don't turn around . . .

Fingers touched my shoulder. I screamed and,
head bent, charged towards the moonlit trees as
fast as I could, before whoever it was could get
a good grip. Then the moon disappeared behind
a cloud and I couldn't see my hand in front of my
face – but I didn't care. If I had to choose between
the dark and the kidnappers, then the dark would
win hands down.

'ANGELA . . . COME BACK HERE . . .'

'WE WON'T HURT YOU . . .'

'DAMN IT! COME BACK . . .'

Their voices seemed to come from everywhere
at once. I couldn't hear their footsteps – the snow
was too deep. For all I knew I might be about to
head-butt one of them in the stomach. Good!

Don't look back, Angela. Keep running.

I heard one of the men shouting something about the phone, but I was too panicky to listen properly. I slipped, then clambered up immediately and kept on running. I ran and ran and ran until I thought my lungs would burst like balloons – and still I kept running. I couldn't hear their voices any more. It didn't matter.

Keep running . . .

And then the ground disappeared. I started falling and falling. I thought I'd never stop.

But I didn't scream.

I must have been knocked out, because I woke up as if from a really bad nightmare – the worst nightmare I'd ever had in my life. Except that it was still dark and bitterly cold – and no dream. My head, my whole body, ached. I couldn't see a thing, but I could sense that something wasn't quite right. I shifted around slightly, feeling about with my hands. There was about forty centimetres of solidness in front of me and after that . . . nothing. I was on a long, thin ledge somewhere and goodness only knew how long the drop was beyond that.

What was left of my courage vanished.

'HELP!' I screamed at the top of my voice. I stretched up and shouted again. 'HELP!'

The ledge moved. I actually felt it vibrate and slip slightly.

I couldn't breathe. I was choking – choking on

45

terror. Slowly, I felt behind me for a handhold. There was none. I was so cold and it was getting worse. I felt so tired. All I wanted to do was sleep. But I remembered Dad telling me once that if you were stuck outside somewhere and really cold, one of the worst things you could do was give in to it and go to sleep.

'Do that and you might never wake up again,' he had said.

I couldn't give up. I *wouldn't*.

Dad . . . If only I could see him one more time – just to hug him and say . . . sorry.

'DAD . . .' I shouted desperately.

'ANGELA? ANGELA!'

And then there was a light shining in my eyes, dazzling me.

'Angela, hang on. I'm here with the police. You've fallen part of the way down Deansea quarry. Stay still. We're coming down to get you.'

I couldn't help it. I started crying again. Sobbing even harder than before. Because it was my dad.

My dad had come to get me.

In the torchlight above, I saw a policeman tie a rope around his waist.

'Angela, I'm Police Sergeant Kent. It's all right. I'm coming to get you, so don't run off, will you!'

That made me laugh a bit, even though I was still crying. Dad and the other policemen and women then held on to the other end of the rope. Sergeant Kent came down for me and lifted me like a sack of potatoes on to his shoulder. Then he climbed back up the quarry face. Dad lifted me off the policeman's back before my feet even touched the ground. I don't know which was tighter – Dad hugging me, or me hugging Dad. My cheek against Dad's was wet, but now I wasn't the one crying. There were three policemen and a policewoman around us, shining torches at us and grinning like Cheshire cats.

'Dad, d–did you give the kidnappers your jewels?' I asked in a whisper.

'Angela, I would have given them everything I had to get you back home safely.' Dad smiled.

'How did you know where to find me?' I sniffed.

'We got to your father just as he was about to leave his shop with two carrier bags filled with jewels. He was able to decipher your cryptic message for us,' said the policeman closest to us.

Dad and I smiled at each other.

'Really, sir, you should have got in touch with us right away,' said Sergeant Kent to Dad. 'We in the police know how to handle things like this.'

'I didn't want to risk it,' Dad said. 'Angela means more to me than all the jewels in the world.'

'Where are the kidnappers?' I asked.

'We've got them all,' said the policewoman.

'They still don't understand how you could have told us about their hideaway when you were blind-folded throughout the drive up here!'

'Why don't you two leave now. Our questions can wait until tomorrow,' said Sergeant Kent.

'Dad, can we go home?' I whispered.

'I'll cook you your favourite dinner while you have a bath and get warm. Then we'll talk. OK?'

'OK.' I grinned. That was all I'd ever wanted.

We walked hand in hand back to Dad's car.

MAELSTROM

by Theresa Breslin

Calum lay stretched out and quiet in his hiding place, and it was his stomach pressed flat against the rough planks which first felt the boat dip as the tide pulled her. There was a strong swell running, from the north-west he reckoned, and he could feel her steady herself to take the first high waves and then move confidently forward in the water. The chug, chug, chug of the engine changed to a deeper throb, in tune with his heartbeats. Then Calum knew that the *Rose of Sharon* had cleared the breakwater and was now heading out to open sea.

He had done it! He raised his head cautiously, brought his knees round sideways and rolled out from underneath the locker in the lower cabin. He could hear the men talking above him. They'd be discussing the best fishing ground to head for, looking up the compass and setting their course. Calum stood up. Better to wait a little while before going on deck. He wanted them to be so far out that there would be no question of turning back when they knew he was on board.

How angry would his uncle be? He remembered the conversation he had overheard weeks ago. His mother speaking softly to Fintry in their kitchen. He was due to sail on the morning tide and Calum had begged to go.

'If I let the boy go with ye,' she had said to her brother-in-law, 'you'd see he came back safe again?'

He had heard his uncle's voice, steady in reply. 'Only the Lord knows when a boat goes out, if it'll be coming home again.' And then, 'If the sea is in him then nothing will ease him until he's a fisherman.'

There was a pause. Calum saw how his mother would be twisting her fingers nervously together.

'I'll leave it for a bit longer.'

He heard the fear in her voice. The fear that had caused his father to sell out his share in the *Rose of Sharon* and take a job ashore. He had decided that night that he would be on the next trip.

He rubbed the dirt from the porthole window and looked out. Dawn was pulling away the dark strands of night and the stars were reflected on a sequined sea. He could see the port lights shining out and the rest of the fleet around them. Ahead of them the *Neptune* and the *Mary Grace*, with the *Lady Caroline* and the *Bonny Lass* off to one side. Soon they would scatter across the face of the sea.

The cabin door opened and one of the crew came in. It was his mother's cousin, Peter.

'Calum!' He shook his head. 'Aye, Fintry always said you'd turn up one day.' He pushed the boy towards the stairs. 'You'd better go and report to the skipper. He's in the wheelhouse.'

On deck in the grey light, Calum felt the boat under his feet move with the sea. He breathed in deeply. This was where he wanted to be. He felt at once vibrantly alive and yet at peace with himself. Ahead of him, in the wheelhouse, he saw his uncle raise his head as he approached. There was no smile of welcome on his face.

'I had to do it this way,' said Calum. And his voice was not pleading. 'She would never let me go.'

'Aye,' said his uncle and he cuffed Calum gently on the head. 'Get some oilskins.' He picked up the handset. 'I'll get on the ship-to-shore to the coast-guard station and ask them to phone down and let them know,' he said, 'afore your mother's wild with worry.'

She should have realized that he would do this eventually. Had to do it. His father would understand, Calum was sure, even though his own life had taken a different course. So different from his brother, softer and rounded where Fintry was bone and muscle. He recalled his uncle working on the boat. His strong, clever fingers coiling the heavy ropes, brown skin, tanned and toughened by sun and wind. His father's hand when he clasped it was soft. Warm, flesh coloured and smooth to touch.

Calum spent every spare minute at the harbour with the fishermen. He was there in the mornings as they unloaded their catch, cascades of fish glittering silver among the crushed ice. He knew every lane and wynd around the port; the old cottages, painted white, pale blue, cream and green, with their red pantiled roofs. The lobster pots and orange nets stretched in front. When he was small he would watch for the *Rose of Sharon* making harbour. Then he had run to meet his uncle, and Fintry would grab him and swing him high among the masts and crying gulls, and placing Calum on his shoulder he would stride home up Shore Road.

And now he was here! Actually on board the *Rose of Sharon* and working as hard as he could to prove, as much to himself as any of the rest, that he could do it. They winched out the nets and he struggled to keep his balance on the wet deck as he ran back and forth at the crew's bidding. This was no sailboat trip, no inshore fishing excursion set up for the summer tourists. The ache in his arms from operating the gear told him this. The sea spray stung his face and salt on his eyelids and his mouth made them sore and raw.

He took his uncle some food and a mug of tea. The radio was tuned to the weather reports. At home Calum always listened to them before falling asleep. After midnight came the close-of-day shipping forecast, a benediction in the night . . .

'Fair Isle, Fastnet and Finisterre – Shannon, Dogger, Rockall and Mallaig . . .'

His own personal evensong, and a link with the boats, far out in the fishing grounds trying to reap their harvest from the sea.

'Attention all shipping. Attention all shipping. The Met Office has issued the following gale warning.'

Fintry put down his half-eaten sandwich, leaned over and turned up the sound.

'. . . three hundred and fifty miles west. Veering west, north-west, wintry showers, storm ten, severe gale nine. Imminent.'

His uncle frowned. 'What d'ye say? Ride it out, or run for home?' Before Calum could answer, the older crewman put his head into the wheelhouse.

'Fintry.' He nodded to the horizon. 'There's a sky building up that I don't like the look of at all.'

'Aye, it's on the wireless. Draw the nets and we'll shelter in for a bit.'

The storm came in quickly, as it often did in those waters. The sky darkened as grey and blue-black cloud came between them and the sun, the wind immediately gusting and alive with malice. The sea rose and became an enemy to be fought, the implacable foe of the deep-sea fisherman.

The boat pitched suddenly as the sea took fretful hold of it and tried to wrench it away from the control of the puny mortal at the wheel. The men acted quickly, moving around Calum, and suddenly he was afraid, very afraid. Yet wasn't this partly why he had come? The danger, the thrill of trying to master the elements?

Andrew, the younger crewman, on his way aft, laughed at the boy's white face. He thumped him on the back.

'I've been in worse,' he said, 'much worse. And that was only on the Millport Ferry.'

The storm rolled and crashed, and now they were in the middle of it. There was a fork of lightning and then blinding, sheeting rain and hail drenched them in moments. The black mast stabbed its finger high, as lightning livid in the dark sky threw it into relief. A monochrome picture seared for ever on Calum's eye.

The boat climbed into a wave. The deck lifted and Calum grabbed for a rail as he lost balance. Higher yet. Now he was almost parallel with the side. Surely they must overturn?

He heard someone laugh, right out loud, and then start to sing.

'Oh, God, our help in ages past . . .' sang Peter. He sounded confident, glorious and unafraid. Calum felt his heart lift. He relaxed his body and went with the movement of the boat as Fintry held her steady and they made headway.

Into the next wave, up and up and up. The world hesitated, trembled, and then they started down again.

Then disaster struck!

Like something from the gates of hell, a lightning ball, intense and terrible, spiralled down from the heavens and struck the mast. It was felled like a rotten tree, crashed past the wheelhouse and down into the hold. The ship's lights, the crackling radio, the singing, all failed into a deadly silence.

For several seconds Calum thought he was the only person alive – on the boat, in the universe. He was aware of a wailing like the keening of some strange animal, and as he put his hands to his mouth to stop his teeth chattering he knew that the sound was coming from him. In utter shock, he moved with great difficulty. He called out. No answer. He tried to make his way forward. But the storm had realized that this boat was now its plaything and threw it carelessly about like a child in a tantrum. He struggled forward and, wriggling under the mast, found himself with his face close to Peter's. He was caught underneath it, his arm crushed and legs twisted horribly. Calum felt the man's death-white face. It was clammy to touch. Then Peter gave a soft moan. He was alive!

Suddenly his uncle was beside him. He ran his hands across Peter's face and body.

'I'll see to him and check on Andrew. You go to the wheelhouse. The radio's down, but try a Mayday. Then take the wheel and try and hold her steady.'

Calum gaped at him, mouth open, stupid.

'DO IT!' snapped Fintry.

Calum got to his feet and staggered into the wheelhouse. The radio was dead. He hit it in anger with the flat of his hand. The wheel was spinning this way and that, as the boat was tossed by the waves and wind. He must try to steer it, he thought, else they would capsize or be swamped. But how and where?

Suddenly there was a beacon in the night, in the black, driving rain ahead of him. What was it? Two flashes, then a pause, two again.

'No,' Calum whispered.

He knew all the lighthouse signalling codes – had memorized them before he was ten years old. The ones around his shoreline he could easily recite. The Taig – two flashes every twenty seconds; the

Point of Inver – one every five. And this one . . . it couldn't be. If it was the Drum then they were off course, and if so close, then in the most deadly danger.

Be calm, he ordered himself. His fingers clenched the wheel. Be precise, as his father would have been. Take care, think carefully. He looked again, staring hard into the darkness, and counted slowly. Where was it and how many? There! Now! A flash. One. Two . . . and then the count in between . . . five, six, seven. It flashed again. Twice. Oh God! It *was* the Drum.

His uncle struggled back into the wheelhouse.

'Andrew's below and unconscious. I've moved some of the weight off Peter's leg. We'll have to make harbour ourself – if we can.' He peered into the darkness. 'I'll need to get a fixing on where we are.'

Calum swallowed to stop himself stuttering.

'I think we're near the rocks at Drum.'

The light sat on the most dangerous part of their coast, perched on a large group of vicious, jagged rocks below high cliffs. With cross-currents in a channel that no craft could master, it was an area which fishermen completely avoided. Now they were caught in it. Cold certainty overwhelmed Calum.

His uncle stared out into the darkness, eyes searching until he saw the beacon. He grunted.

'Aye, it's the Drum all right. I should have known you'd not make a mistake.' He pulled a chart down.

Calum bent his head on the wheel. They were doomed, all of them. He and his uncle would be smashed with the boat on the rocks, while Peter, the most experienced of them all, who most likely knew exactly what was happening, lay frustrated and helpless, to be drowned like a kitten in a bag. Calum's grasp slackened and the wheel spun quickly through his fingers.

'Keep that wheel right!' his uncle yelled.

Calum gazed back at him. 'It's hopeless,' he said.

His uncle flung the chart aside and gripped Calum fiercely by his shoulders. 'It's never hopeless,' he shouted. 'Your father's been the lifeboat cox for twenty years. D'ye think he ever turned back when things were at their worst? How many folk would have drowned if he had given up? You always wanted to be a sailor. Now be one, and steer the damn boat!'

He picked up the chart. 'If we're going to strike, at least we might choose where and how. There's a point where the channel lies close to the shore, where the cliffs are not so high. Now the tide's out for another hour. If we can run her aground there, then we might come out of this . . .'

Calum and his uncle fought to get control of the boat. She was being pulled by the currents, corkscrewing violently in the maelstrom. As she was pushed nearer and closer in to the cliffs, Calum realized that sailing this way she would be driven straight on to the rocks. He saw in his mind the water flooding in as her back was broken on the reef. He understood now what his uncle had said. If they could bring her about, perhaps the damage would not be so bad. He dragged on the wheel, and she responded heavily. He moved his hands across and, bracing himself against the frame of the wheelhouse, he hauled on the wheel as hard as he could.

'Good man!' his uncle cried. 'She's coming round!'

Calum felt the run of the current take her. Could they keep her side on and guide her past the high reef? His arms, shoulders and back were aching. Sweat streaked his face as he desperately tried to steer the boat while some demon grappled her away from him.

They almost had her straightened up when, with a great grinding, tearing crash, she struck. He was thrown to the floor and then out across the deck as the boat canted violently to one side, held fast in the teeth of the rocks.

Calum got to his feet, blood pouring from a cut on his forehead. He was dizzy and sick and fought down nausea as he tried to assess the damage. She was holed, and badly, but, praise God, it was above the waterline. He ran back to his uncle.

'Take this.' Fintry wound a rope around Calum's waist and made it fast to the rail. 'Tell them at the station we need a helicopter to bring a line aboard, and a tug standing by to pull us off. They'll have to move fast. If the tide turns and we're still here, we'll be pounded to pieces.' He held the boy by his shoulders. 'Good luck.' Then he pulled Calum towards him and hugged him. He stepped back into the wheelhouse. 'Go.' he said.

Calum went back out on deck. They were very close in. A treacherous scramble would take him across to the shingle below. He pulled off his oilskins, hesitated and then discarded his lifejacket. It would only restrict him, and anyway . . . He regarded the raging sea only a metre or so away from him. If he fell in there, he doubted whether the lifejacket would be of any use.

He lowered himself from the raised side of the boat, slipped on the rocks and fell at once into the water. Immediately, the intense cold penetrated through to his bones. He swallowed salt water and, for a crazy moment, almost felt like laughing. There were about six different ways to perish at sea and it looked as if he was going to experience all of them. Then a great grey towering wave lifted him and threw him on to the tiny beach. He staggered to his feet, was violently sick and then sat down again quickly. He was dizzy and blinded with blood from the wound in his head. He would need to take time to think.

He thought of his father again. He did things slowly, carefully. The little wooden ships which he lovingly fashioned from wood and sold to the holidaymakers. He took time and patience with his models. He didn't make mistakes. Calum untied the rope and pulled the tail of his shirt from under his jacket and tore off some material. He wrapped a bandage firmly round his head, then he pulled off the heavy rubber sea boots. He tore more strips and wrapped them round his socks and then a piece around each hand. He rubbed himself furiously all over to warm himself. Then he stood up and walked purposefully towards the cliff path.

The wind was howling around him, anxious to pluck him away from the fragile hold he had on the scrub and gorse. He was almost on his hands and knees as he followed the track higher and higher. The sea boiled below him, and he imagined himself falling and his skull cracked open like a gull's egg on the rocks below.

At one point a bird flew out, screeching at his head, and he had to rest until his heart stopped thumping and his legs ceased trembling. His hands and feet were cut and bruised when he finally levered himself over the top edge. The coastguard station was about two miles round the headland.

Legs shaking and tears running down his face, Calum picked himself up from the rough grass and started to run.

'Hot drink. Bath. Bed,' his mother ordered after the doctor had left Calum's bedroom.

Calum tried to get up. His legs and arms were bruised and sore. His voice wavered.

'I have to see Fintry,' he said, 'and Peter and Andrew.'

'They're fine.' His father came into the room carrying a tray. 'I've spoken to the matron at the cottage hospital. They are going to be all right.'

'And—'

'The *Rose of Sharon* is safe in harbour.' His father smiled at him. 'Now rest, and we'll visit them in the morning.'

'I won't give up the sea,' said Calum as they entered the hospital the next day.

'No,' said his father, 'and you shouldn't either. It was different for me. I was following a family tradition, but my heart wasn't in it. Your mother could see that. I didn't love the sea the way Fintry does . . . the way you do.'

He held out his hands, palms up, and looked down at them. 'We each do according to how we are.'

Calum walked down the ward to his uncle's bed.

'She's safe,' he told him. 'She needs a bit of work, but the *Rose of Sharon* will put to sea again.'

'Calum's quite a hero, now,' his mother said.

'No,' said Fintry quietly. He took Calum's hands firmly in his own. 'He's a fisherman.'

THE PAINTBRUSH WARRIOR
by Jonathan Kebbe

For a moment more all was still, a warm breeze whispering through the shanty town of La Colina, Pepe fast asleep . . . then all at once the night exploded, the front door caved in, the tin house shook and Pepe sat bolt upright, thinking another earthquake had struck. Beside him on the mattress, his elder brother Roberto knew what was happening and leapt up to try and escape. Too late. Boots thundered through the house, soldiers tore down the curtain that served as bedroom walls, cornered Roberto in their torchbeams and shouted, 'We've got him!'

Flashlights blinded Pepe, a soldier grabbed him by the hair. 'Leave him!' barked a sergeant. 'He's only a kid.'

Mother was screaming, his sister Maria threw

65

herself at the soldiers, but they punched her and dragged Roberto to the street. Throwing him to the ground, they tied his hands and flung him into a truck, where more soldiers stood on the backs of other young men and women. Eighteen-year-old Roberto was the lead artist of a wall-painting brigade of young people, who painted cartoons three metres high on walls in the city, denouncing the terrible military dictatorship. Now they were all captured.

The army truck roared away, leaving police Captain Alfredo Díaz standing in the street, hands on hips, looking up and down as if to say, 'Let that be a lesson to you all.' Boarding a jeep, he was driven off in a swirl of dust.

Mother collapsed and Pepe and Maria tried to comfort her. In all probability, Roberto and his comrades would never be seen again. The generals didn't believe in trials. Anyone who stood in their way was crushed like an insect. Mama couldn't bear it – first her husband, now her son. One minute she was strong, handsome, auburn-haired; the next, grey, stooped and silent. Maria was mostly away, employed as a maid by a family in town, so Pepe, aged eleven, became the man of the house, living with grandmother and the ghost of his mother, who wandered the streets collecting cardboard to sell for a few pesos. The leaves blew, the frosts came, and every night Pepe lay and cried beside Roberto's empty space.

One warm summer's evening, a year after Roberto disappeared, Pepe and best friend Diego were in the city centre as usual, trying to make money. Now and then a rich man sat down on the rim of the fountain, and Diego would root in his box of polishes and furiously clean the man's shoes. Pepe, who took after his brother, drew pictures on the pavement with coloured chalk supplied by a kind teacher at school. His Madonna and Child was so eye-catching that people stopped to admire it, and his plastic cup brimmed over with coins.

'I'm knackered,' said Pepe. 'Let's go.'

'I haven't made enough,' Diego replied. 'My papa will kill me.'

'Don't worry, you can have some of mine.'

'Look!' Diego interrupted. In a side street, police were pointing at a huge cartoon splashed across the rear of a cinema, depicting the hated dictator, General Pinochet, stamping on the word DEMOCRACIA. 'Want to know a secret?' Diego whispered. '*Our* brigade did that.'

'What! But they were all caught with Roberto.'

'A new brigade! We did it last night.'

'*That*'s why you fell asleep in school,' laughed Pepe. 'Can I come along next time?'

'Maybe when you're older.'

'But *you're* only twelve.'

'Ah, but I can climb trees and roofs. They call me Monkey – I'm the lookout.'

Pepe tried to hide his disappointment. 'That cartoon's useless! Roberto was much better.'

Pepe had a point; the drawing of the dictator was amateurish, comical. 'Know something?' Diego reflected. 'You'd do much better.'

'Look out!' Pepe warned.

While his men scaled ladders to scrub the cartoon from the wall, Captain Díaz, unmistakable with his cruel hooked nose and moustache, was crossing the square. 'Why are you shaking, boy?' he shouted.

'It's getting chilly, *capitán*,' said Diego.

'Clean my boots so I can see my face in them.'

'Why, with a face like that?' muttered Pepe under his breath, chuckling fearfully to himself. But when he looked up from his drawing, Captain Díaz was staring at him, and all the time Diego rubbed and polished, Captain Díaz stared at Pepe. Even when he stood up and paid Diego, he had eyes only for Pepe. 'What's your name?' he asked.

Pepe added one more golden curl to Mother Mary's head and looked up. 'Me, *señor*? Pepe.'

'Stand up, boy, when I talk to you.'

While Pepe stood straight and looked him in

the eye, Captain Díaz studied Pepe's face, his dark curling hair and long-lashed eyes. 'How old are you?'

'Twelve, *señor*.'

'Twelve . . .' the policeman repeated in a strange, dreamy, bitter tone, as if angry with Pepe for being alive when someone close to him was gone. He never looked at his boots, nor at Pepe's art. Turning abruptly on his heels, he walked away.

When they returned by bus to La Colina, Diego was afraid to go home, even with the extra coins Pepe gave him, so they ran to their hideout, a burned-out van on the wasteland, and played draughts until the white pieces glowed like eyes in the dark. Then Pepe accompanied Diego home. When Diego's mother was alive, home was much like Pepe's, a hovel leaning into the wind, cheered up by flowerpots in the mud yard. Now it had windowpanes, armchairs, colour TV and gas fires. His father made good money, though no-one knew how. Asleep in front of the TV, with empty beer bottles by his outstretched bad leg, Señor Calvo opened one bleary eye.

'Where you been?'

'Working, papá.'

'Let me see.' Diego emptied his pockets and his father counted. 'Not bad, but could be better. Make your friend some tea.'

'My grandmother's waiting,' Pepe thanked him, and left.

But he didn't go far. Pausing outside the door he heard, 'Come here, you little swine. I'll teach you . . .'

Peering through the window he saw Señor Calvo hobble after Diego like a circus act, catching him by the scruff of the neck. 'How am I to feed five brats when you do nothing, when you tell me nothing, give me no information to sell?' he bellowed, shaking Diego and slapping him until he cried. Then they folded into each other's arms and wept together.

Worried about Diego, puzzled by what he'd overheard, Pepe slipped away.

Winter returned, sleet turned the roads of La Colina to rivers of mud, and one day Pepe came out of school to find the leaders of the new brigade waiting for him.

'Do you want to avenge Roberto?' demanded ferocious, bearded Julio.

'Yes.'

'Are you brave enough to take his place?' challenged Valentina, gazing at him with her huge startling eyes.

'Yes.'

'Then tell your good grandmother we want you.'

★

A week later, Pepe was at the front door when the truck pulled up. 'Mamá, I have to go out.'

Mother was scrubbing the table for the tenth time.

'Mamá . . .?' Pepe caught his grandmother's eye, and ran to his room to pull Roberto's brushes from under the mattress. A knock came on the door, and Valentina stood there. 'Problems?' she said.

Pepe's heart turned over. Though she was twenty, he thought her beautiful, with her vivid eyes and jet-black hair tied in a bright headband. 'I'm ready,' he said.

His grandmother turned him round, held his face, pressed her cracked lips to his brow like a protective spell. Then to the young woman in the doorway she said, 'You'll be careful, *señorita*?'

'Our lives depend on it.'

'Where are you going?' his mother enquired absently.

'I won't be long, mamá.'

The truck roared, hands reached out under canvas to haul Pepe in like a fish. His heart soared, riding into town to take on the generals with Roberto's brushes in his fist. 'I can hardly believe it!' he whispered, squeezing next to Diego in the dark.

'What are *you* doing here?'

'They didn't tell you? They're trying me out. I

71

practised all yesterday. Isn't it great – going into battle together!'

But Diego only looked away. What's up with him? Pepe wondered. He's jealous – to hell with him! But as he peered out at the moon sailing over the mountains, he began to feel uneasy about his friend.

Rumbling into Santiago, the truck turned off a splendid *avenida*, with its mansions and flashy cars, and took lonely side streets to reach a quiet square dominated by Iglesia de San Antonio. No ordinary church, it was the one the generals attended on Sundays in a show of Christian goodness.

'Pepe,' Diego hissed as they jumped down, 'I've a bad feeling about tonight. Keep your eyes peeled and run like hell if you see anything.'

'Don't worry!' Pepe slapped his back. 'It's going to be great!'

A side door of the church had been left open by a sympathetic priest, and while Diego crept inside and climbed guiltily to the belfry, Pepe, dizzy with excitement, stepped up to the church wall, plunged his brother's brush in black paint and set to work. His task was to compose quick, clear outlines for the others to fill in with bright colours, and he began by dashing off the gigantic shoes of the general. Hoisted on Julio's shoulders, he sketched the military trousers. By now the stepladders were in place, and he was climbing more than two metres

off the ground and, balancing on a plank, started on the general's jacket, complete with epaulettes and sash. While the rest of the brigade swarmed over the wall, Pepe plucked a finer brush from his back pocket to trace helpless figures wriggling in the fists of the giant. Finally he painted a skeleton's head on the dictator's shoulders, with dark glasses and a terrible grin.

But before he could finish, Pepe was surprised by a glimmer of light reflected in a stained-glass window and, turning his head, he glimpsed a number of darkened vehicles creeping through side streets, the moon catching their mirrors. The army!

Just then he heard Diego cry, 'Look out!' from the belfry. Too late. As the brigade scattered, headlights streamed into the square, flinging Pepe's shadow high against the church wall.

By the time the army reached the church, there was no-one near the ladders, the brigade was sitting innocently in the truck, and two members were in the road, pretending to fix the engine.

'Nothing to do with us,' said Julio.

'Liar!' growled the police captain.

'We've been to market,' Valentina explained, 'and broke down.'

A rifle butt struck her, another crashed into Julio's legs, and both collapsed in the road.

Inside the candle-lit church, Pepe crouched on the floor of a confessional listening to the shouting, praying he wouldn't hear shooting and wondering how it was that so many police arrived at once – almost as if . . .

Then he recalled Diego's strange behaviour and warning, and what he'd overheard his father saying: *How can I feed us when you tell me nothing, when you give me no information to sell?* All at once he understood and, shaking with fear, he vowed that if he survived he'd go after Diego's blood, even if Diego was bigger and stronger.

Suddenly he heard the church door open and footfalls on the tiles, working their way up one aisle and turning to start slowly down the aisle where he was hiding. The steps came closer . . . closer, and now he could make out the darting beam of a flashlight probing the darkness. He heard the steps stop at the next confessional, heard a door squeak, the searcher shining his torch and finding nothing. Steps came again, scuffing the tiles in front of his hideout. Pressing his head between his knees he squeezed up tight and held his breath. He heard leather squeaking, a pistol being drawn, then the door opened, a beam brushed the floor, found his feet and played at will over his body. Heart hammering, he braced himself. Mamá, help me! he wanted to cry, but nothing came out, and a toecap slid between his knees and lifted his chin. Opening his eyes, he was blinded by torchlight.

'What are you doing, boy?' The voice was

deep and strong and vaguely familiar. 'Stand.'

As Pepe got up, his brushes clattered to the floor.

'The truth, boy.'

'I painted the picture outside, *señor*.'

'You? Look at me.'

The light was removed from his eyes, and he recognized Captain Díaz by his nose and moustache.

'Haven't I seen you before? Pepe, isn't it?'

'Yes, *capitán*,' he blurted, remembering the strange scene in town when the captain couldn't keep his eyes off him, as if Pepe reminded him of someone else. He was gazing at Pepe now, pointing the pistol at his chest, a mournful look in his eye.

'*Capitán?*' a voice echoed through the church. 'Need any help?'

Still the captain stared. 'No, Sergeant.'

'Find anything?'

Pepe gazed up into the captain's face, and saw tears welling in his eyes.

'No, Sergeant.'

Captain Díaz left. Outside he looked at the row of young men and women lying face down in the road, hands tied behind their backs. Normally he would arrest the lot. After days of torture, they would be killed. But to the amazement of his men, he ordered them freed. 'God help you if I ever catch you again.'

In the truck on the way home, between tears and laughter, they praised Diego for raising the alarm. Pepe held his tongue, shaking with emotion, grateful for Valentina's arm around his shoulders. 'Fantastic picture, Pepe,' she whispered. 'Roberto would be proud.'

When they reached La Colina, Diego slipped away before Pepe could catch him. Next day Diego wasn't in school, and after dark Pepe went after him, iron bar in hand, bent on cracking his skull. Diego's father opened the door.

'It was you, wasn't it?' Pepe pointed the weapon at him. 'You're a *sapo*, aren't you? A police informer. That's how you make your rotten money!'

'Who do you think you're talking to?' Señor Calvo bared his teeth and closed his fist. 'I could break you in little—'

'If I was to tell Valentina and Julio . . .'

Señor Calvo went pale and caught hold of the door frame.

'They'd come looking for you, wouldn't they?'

'Don't, Pepe, I beg you. The cops forced me. I'll never—'

'Where's Diego?'

'I haven't seen him, we're all looking.'

Pepe ran. The lanes were frozen and puddles cracked underfoot; the moon raced him across the wasteland. He ran until he saw a faint glow in the distance, then walked towards the hideout. Smoke was curling from its roof and, as he approached, he heard the strains of a tin whistle. When he peered in, there was Diego huddled in the corner round a fire. Pepe leapt aboard brandishing the iron bar. 'You're dead, Diego.'

Diego jumped up, snatched a smouldering plank and flourished it.

'You, you little runt, you couldn't kill a mouse!'

'*Sapo* . . .' Pepe breathed, closing in, slowly swinging the bar. 'Coward . . . traitor . . . you could have got Valentina and all the rest killed. You're worse than the solders. I'd rather be dead than be you . . .'

'No, Pepe, listen.' Diego backed away round the fire. He'd never seen Pepe like this, so calm and cruel and fearless. 'I couldn't help it—'

'Don't give me that—'

'I couldn't! Papa's a drunk. He's mad, he keeps crying about my mother. He beats me. I had to help him. I hate myself, I can't stand it any more. I'm never going back – I'll live with you if you let me—'

'You? A *sapo*! In my house?' Pepe laughed scornfully. 'I never want to see you again.' Flinging the bar on the floor, he stormed out.

'Pepe!' Diego called after him. Pepe kept walking. 'Pepe! Don't go, please!'

As Pepe marched on, with Diego's cries echoing

78

after him, he thought how strange it was that Diego gave a warning from the belfry when he wasn't meant to, and how Captain Díaz had shown mercy when *he* wasn't meant to. His pace slackened; he stopped. It was dark all around, and silent now.

He turned slowly. Diego was standing in the back of the van, silhouetted by the fire, shoulders shaking. They stood gazing at one another across the darkness.

ANGELS
by Judith O'Neill

Ben woke to find himself lying on a white sandy beach under a blazing sun. His whole body ached. His blue shirt and trousers were stiff with dried salt water. His feet were bare. For a few bewildered minutes he remembered nothing, but then in a rush it all came back to him. The instant when their ship had struck a reef in the dark; wild screams as the terrified immigrants shoved their way towards the lifeboats; a sudden lurch as the ship rolled over and sank; his own leap into the sea, a cork lifebelt around his waist, cold water gurgling in his throat. And then the long, long struggle to the shore.

Ben lifted his head. There was no sign of the ship out to sea. Not even one floating mast or a sail. The beach was empty too, apart from a bun-

dle of sodden clothes right by the water's edge. He
crawled awkwardly over the hot sand till he reached
the bundle. Cautiously, he poked at it. He shivered.
Someone was there, inside those wet clothes! Alive
or dead? He dragged the bundle away from the
water and rolled it over. A thin waif of a girl
opened her eyes and stared up at him.

'Who are you?' she asked.

'Ben Stevenson,' he answered, looking down
at her white face, her drenched black hair. The
girl seemed to be about his own age though much
smaller.

'Where's Kathleen?' she murmured. 'Kathleen
and Mary?'

'Who?' asked Ben.

'Me two big sisters, Kathleen and Mary. We all
jumped from the ship at the same time. I couldn't
find them in the dark. Where are they?'

Ben didn't like to say they were probably
drowned. He tried to sound more confident than
he really felt.

'We're the only ones on *this* beach,' he said.
'Probably the others have been washed up further
along the coast. What's your name? I didn't ever
see you on the ship.'

'I was there all right and I saw you often
enough. I'm Bridie Flanagan from Dublin.'

Ben gasped.

'Not one of those skinny Irish orphans down

on the bottom deck!' he said, his voice shocked. He edged away from her.

'I'm Irish all right,' said Bridie proudly. 'And what's wrong with that? But I'm not an orphan! They just call us orphans because they took us from the workhouse to the ship. Me mother had to put us in the workhouse when me father died. What else could she do? When we find a fine new family to look after us in Australia, then we'll soon be sending the money home for me mother to come out and join us.'

Ben laughed at her. He couldn't stop himself. He pushed both his hands through his fair hair so that it stood up around his head and he laughed out loud. He looked utterly amazed.

'There'll be no fine new family for you in Australia, Bridie Flanagan! Whatever gave you that idea? You'll be hired out to work for some rich gentleman and his wife in the country. You'll be slaving and scrubbing in some homestead, miles from anywhere! And miles from those sisters of yours, too!'

'How do you know?' she asked suspiciously, sitting upright on the sand and glaring at Ben.

'My father told me. He's the surgeon on the ship. You must know which one he is. The big tall man with a black beard. He says you Irish orphans are the skinniest children he's ever seen in his whole life. Half-starved, he reckons you are!

He says you're all being shipped out to the colony
to be servants.'

'Where is he, this father of yours who knows
so much?' demanded Bridie.

Ben was silent for a minute.

'I don't know,' he said. 'He put this lifebelt
around me and then the ship began to go down.
I never saw him again.'

To Bridie's astonishment, the boy began to
cry. All her anger melted away.

'He'll be all right,' she said kindly. 'Prob'ly
he's found me sisters already, Kathleen and Mary,
and he's looking after them right this minute. And
your mother'll be making them all a wonderful
meal.'

'I haven't got a mother,' sobbed Ben, crying
louder still. 'She's dead! There's just my father
and me!'

'I'm sorry,' said Bridie gently. 'I shouldn't have
said that. I didn't know at all. Now we'd better
be going to look for your father and me two big
sisters. Come on!'

Bridie jumped up and smoothed her long wet
dress. She tried to smile at Ben, but he couldn't
smile back.

'Which way should we go?' he mumbled, avoid-
ing her eyes and brushing away the tears with the
backs of his hands.

Bridie had no idea. She looked one way along

the beach to a line of sand–dunes, rising and falling into the distance. She looked the other way to a high yellow cliff curving around the bay. She looked inland to a forest of dark trees.

'We'd better go that way,' she said, pointing to the trees. 'We'll have to get some shelter from this terrible sun.'

'But we should stay near the sea,' said Ben, frowning. 'We're more likely to find someone to help us if we stick to the sea. Someone from the ship. Or whalers. My father says there are whaling settlements along this coast. And sheep-runs, too. If we keep walking close to the sea, we're sure to find someone.'

'Well, let's get under those trees first. We needn't go too far from the sea. So long as we can hear it, we'll be all right.'

'You're very bossy for an orphan!' protested Ben.

'I told you. I'm not an orphan at all. You're the orphan, not me!'

Ben was shocked into silence. She could be right.

'Are you going to be a servant too?' she asked, looking at him in genuine interest. 'We might work for the same family. You could be out in the stables and I'd be in the kitchen.'

'No!' shouted Ben, suddenly angry. 'Don't be ridiculous! I'm not going to be a servant! I'll be going to school in Melbourne. The very best school, my father says. We'll be buying a grand new house right in the centre of town. The colony needs doctors, you see. My father's a famous doctor from London.'

'He *was* a famous doctor!' said Bridie.

Ben felt uncomfortable. No-one had ever spoken to him so sharply before. And she was nothing but an Irish servant-girl! At home he wouldn't ever have had to speak to such a skivvy, and here he was, stranded with her in this strange country! He decided to take charge before she started bossing him any more.

'Come on,' he said briskly. 'We'll get to the trees first and then we'll turn west towards the setting sun. We'll keep those sand-dunes to our left and we'll never let them out of our sight.'

'I'm thirsty,' said Bridie.

'Well, look out for water,' snapped Ben, and he strode off ahead of her towards the dark line of trees. He wasn't used to walking without shoes. The sand burnt the soles of his feet; sharp twigs scratched him; the pebbles pressed hard against his soft white toes. He limped. Glancing back over his shoulder he was surprised to see Bridie walking more easily on her stick-like legs than he did on his own strong plump ones. He couldn't understand it.

The trees, when they reached them at last, were an odd shape, quite unlike any trees at home. Their narrow grey-green leaves hung downwards;

their high branches were ragged and untidy; their scent was strong and unfamiliar. A flock of bright red parrots flew noisily from branch to branch. At least the shade was cool.

'Water!' shrieked Bridie in excitement and crouched by a tiny pool lying in the curve of a rock. Ben flopped down beside her.

'Let me have some too!' he said. Their two parched tonges lapped at the water till the rock-pool was empty.

As the sun moved steadily down the western sky, Ben and Bridie plodded on under the trees, the sand-dunes always to their left and the sea roaring faintly from beyond the dunes. Hunger began to prick and stab at their stomachs. Their pace slowed. Bridie chewed a handful of leaves but the taste was bitter. She spat.

'I want to sleep,' she said.

'But it's not night-time yet,' protested Ben. 'We've got to keep moving while it's still light.'

'I'll move tomorrow,' she said with a laugh, and she lay down on the wiry grass. She fell asleep at once.

Ben slept only fitfully even after darkness fell. Time and again he woke suddenly to hear some heavy animal moving about under the trees, breathing and snuffling. He heard a mournful night-bird calling. He saw a sky full of brilliant stars overhead. He even thought he heard voices. Voices whispering in words he couldn't understand. Voices laughing. Then all was silent and he slept again.

Bridie was the first to wake when the sun came up. The bush was ringing with birdsong. Close by her head lay a round dish of bark, full to the brim with water. Unbelieving, she put out one hand to touch it. She sipped at the water. It was cool and fresh.

'Ben! Ben! Just look at this! The holy angels themselves are looking after us!'

Ben woke with a start, half hearing her words.

'My father doesn't believe in angels!' he said primly. Then he saw the water in its bark dish. His face flushed in sudden surprise. He snatched up the dish and drank. He passed it to Bridie.

At that moment, Ben's eye was caught by three sticks lying on the ground. Three sticks laid out carefully in the shape of an arrow. They pointed away from the sea and deeper into the heart of the forest. He hoped Bridie hadn't seen them. He didn't want to go that way. He tried to hurry her on, but she leapt on the sticks with delight.

'It's those holy angels!' she cried. 'First they bring us water and then they put a sign here to guide us! Come on, Ben, this is the way!'

Bridie plunged into the wild bush country, running ahead through the thick undergrowth of fern and sapling. She kept in the lead for hours, muttering happily about angels every time she came across another arrow of sticks. Ben dragged himself along a little behind her, looking back longingly towards the sea. He couldn't even hear the breakers now. He felt scared.

Suddenly a great animal leapt out right in front of them, hopping gracefully through the bush on its strong back legs and the thrust of a powerful tail. It stopped and gazed at Bridie and Ben. They gazed back, too astonished to cry out. The creature bounded slowly away.

'M-my f-father told me about them!' stammered Ben. 'K-k-kangaroos!'

'Will they hurt us?'

Ben shook his head. He could bear his terrible hunger no longer. He pulled some pods from the nearest plant and wolfed down the brown seeds. Bridie dragged a thin white root from the ground and sank her teeth into the flesh. Nothing tasted good. Everything tasted strange. But any food was better than no food at all and it seemed to do them no harm. With torn clothes, tangled hair, scratched faces and bleeding feet they staggered on from arrow to arrow all through the long hot day.

The next morning, as Bridie stretched out her hand to a new bark dish of water lying close by her head, she smelt smoke. She sniffed at the air.

'Where there's smoke, there's people! Come on, Ben!'

She drank her share of the water, passed the dish to Ben and waited only till he had finished drinking. Then she hurtled off between the tall trees, following the scent of smoke. Sometimes the smoke seemed closer, sometimes further off. Once or twice they even thought they saw it, drifting white above the forest, but it was always moving on ahead of them like a will-o'-the-wisp.

'Angels on fire, I suppose,' sneered Ben, staggering along behind Bridie. He pushed himself to overtake her, to walk right out in front, to be the leader, but he could never manage it. Her feet seemed harder than his and her skinny legs seemed tougher. He groaned out loud in fury as they wandered further and further away from the sea.

Just then, through a curtain of dripping tree ferns, they stumbled on a broad, deep creek. Somehow the sound and the sight of all that rushing, bubbling water made Ben feel a bit better. He lowered himself stiffly into the creek and lay right down on the pebbly bed near the bank, to let the water soothe his aching legs and back, his burning arms and feet. He washed his face and poured handfuls of water over his head till his hair was clean. Bridie would have none of it. She drank her fill and then simply sat nervously on the edge and watched him.

'How do we get across?' she asked, looking fearfully over to the trees on the other side.

Ben pointed to the flat stones dotted here and there in the creek.

'We jump from one stone to the next,' he said.

'I can't,' said Bridie, her face whiter than ever, her fingers clenched.

'It's easy,' said Ben, and he pulled himself on to his feet and began to leap from stone to stone till he stood on the far side, grinning back at her in triumph.

'You go on ahead!' she called across to him. 'I'm scared of water. I'll just wait here till you find someone.'

'Scared of water!' Ben bellowed back at her. 'How could you be scared of water?'

'Everyone's scared of something!' she called, tears pricking in her eyes.

'Those angels you keep talking about'll help you!' shouted Ben scornfully. 'You know I can't go on ahead by myself. We've got to stick together. Come on! The smoke smells much stronger over here. We must be nearly there.'

Bridie shook her head. How could she possibly tell him at the top of her voice about the cruel black water in the river at home? The river where her little brother Patrick had drowned only last year, though she'd tried to pull him out in time. Nothing in the world would persuade her to cross this creek!

Ben waited and waited. Bridie sat still. At last he came back to her, stepping lightly from stone to stone, jumping over the wider gaps where the water ran deep and swirled noisily around the rocks. When he reached her again, she was crying.

'I'll help you,' said Ben, his scorn vanishing at once.

'How?'

'I'll carry you.'

Bridie stopped crying and laughed.

'You couldn't carry me! You can hardly walk!'

'Get up on my back and we'll see,' he said.

Rather to his surprise, she did exactly as he asked. He bent over and she slowly climbed on to his back and put her arms tight, too tight, around his neck. She gripped him in a vice of terror. She sobbed under her breath, 'The water! The water!'

Ben stepped cautiously on to the first stone. With both arms fully stretched out to balance himself, he moved carefully on to the next, and then to the next, his wet foot slipping a little each time till he made it firm. When the gap between stones was too wide for his legs to reach, he went straight down into the creek itself, feeling carefully for the pebbles at the bottom, the water rising well over his knees.

Bridie shrieked and squirmed.

'Keep still, Bridie! Keep still!' he begged her.

Back on the flat stones now, he was almost across. With a final staggering leap he flew over the last deep channel to the bank. Bridie loosened her fierce grip and slid to the ground. She was laughing and crying at the same time.

'You're an angel yourself, Ben Stevenson!' she said.

Ben went red with embarrassment, but he felt rather pleased with himself all the same.

The smoke was certainly stronger here. Ben and Bridie moved forwards slowly, side by side, sniffing hopefully at the smoky air and calling out loudly as they went.

'Help! Help! Is anyone there? We're lost!'

Suddenly there came the cheerful sound of an axe biting into wood. The sound of voices through the trees. A baby's cry.

'Help!' bawled Bridie, louder than ever as she ran full-tilt into a clearing in the bush. She and Ben stopped. There in front of them was a cluster of bark shelters. A circle of laughing black faces around a smoking fire. A clump of long spears propped against a tree. A tall grey-haired woman brandishing a fire-stick in her hand. She wore nothing but a skimpy piece of red cloth around her waist.

'Whitefeller   piccaninnies!'   announced   the

woman, smiling down at them from a broad shining face.

'They're black!' stammered Bridie to Ben in astonishment. 'And they've got no proper clothes on!'

'A–a–aborigines,' stuttered Ben. 'My f–f–father says . . .'

'But what are they doing here?'

'They think it's their country.'

'Perhaps it is!' whispered Bridie. 'I'm off!' and she turned to run. The tall woman was quicker. She sprang forward and grabbed Bridie's arm. Bridie screamed. The woman laughed and loosened her grip.

'No cry, piccaninny,' she said. 'Blackfellers help you. No hurt you.'

The voice was kind. Bridie stopped yelling. The woman led Bridie towards the fire where fish were cooking, each pierced by a clean green stick. And there, right beside the fire, lay a familiar bark dish, full to the brim with clear creek water. Bridie gasped. She pointed to the dish and then up at the woman. The woman nodded. Bridie scratched an arrow on the dry ground and looked up again at the woman, raising her eyebrows in a silent question. The woman nodded and smiled. Bridie smiled back at her in relief.

'It's all right, Ben,' she said. 'They're friends!'

'Angels!' murmured Ben, laughing to himself

as he stretched out eager hands to take the fish the woman was offering him.

The aborigines – men, women and children – gathered close around Ben and Bridie and watched them as they gnawed at the fish in desperate hunger. A child put out a hand to stroke Ben's torn shirt, to feel Bridie's tangled hair. Everyone was laughing.

That night Ben and Bridie slept soundly, sheltered by a bark hut. Early the next morning the tall woman was awake before them.

'Come!' she said. 'Find plenty whitefeller!'

They followed her through the bush for an hour till they came to a wide rutted track cut through the trees. In the soft earth, Ben saw the clear fresh prints of a horseshoe.

'Horses, Bridie! But where?'

The tall black woman pointed to the left along the track. Ben was almost running now. His stiff legs had new life in them. He stumbled and fell, spread-eagled on the track, his ankle twisted under him. To Bridie's astonishment, the woman picked him up easily and heaved him on to her back. So Ben was carried up the last long hill to the bark hut where a young white woman, a baby straddling her hip, was feeding hens in a fenced yard.

'Missus!' their guide called out to her. 'Piccaninnies!'

The young woman looked up and caught sight first of Ben sliding to the ground, and then of

Bridie. She put down her baby on the grass and ran towards them. She hugged them almost as if they were her own long-lost children.

'Wandering in the bush!' she said. 'Who are you? Where have you been?'

Ben explained.

'The shipwreck!' gasped the young woman. 'The *Killarney*!'

Ben and Bridie nodded.

'I heard the news from one of the other shepherds yesterday. There's a few of you poor people been rescued in a lifeboat further down the coast. And others washed up drowned.'

'Mary and Kathleen?' asked Bridie anxiously.

'I don't know,' said the woman, wishing she hadn't said so much. 'I'm sorry, dear. I've heard no names at all. But when my Jim's back with the sheep this afternoon, he'll be sure to ride down to the whaling settlement to find out for you. Come inside now, and we'll eat. I'll find you some decent clothes to put on, too. You do look a strange sight, the pair of you.'

Bridie gazed at Ben and he at her. They couldn't help laughing at themselves. They looked around for the tall black woman to thank her, but she had gone already, melting back into the bush. Ben limped into the hut. The young woman put her baby into Bridie's arms.

'You look as if you'd be good with children,' she said.

'I am!' said Bridie proudly, trying not to think about Patrick slipping away from her in the black water. 'I always looked after the little ones at home.'

Jim set off for the whaling settlement just before sunset. It was midnight before he was back. Ben and Bridie sat up in their beds in the wall as he came inside the hut with his lantern burning.

'There's a doctor safe and sound,' he announced. 'By the name of Stevenson. Out of his mind with grief over his son. Is that you, lad?'

'Yes!' breathed Ben. 'That's me!'

'And there's six poor little Irish girls got to the shore somehow,' Jim went on. 'I don't know how they did it. They must be tougher than they look. Two of them were asking for you, Bridie. They couldn't stop crying, the two of them, when I told them you were safe with us. Mary and Kathleen Flanagan they're called.'

Bridie gave a whoop of joy and sprang from her bed. She rushed to Jim the shepherd and hugged his long legs in relief. She was crying too and calling out for her sisters.

'The angels!' she sobbed. 'The angels looked after them!'

'Humph!' snorted Ben with a smile, but he couldn't help wondering if perhaps she was right after all.

SAM'S STORM

by Douglas Hill

Sam stormed out of the cottage, slamming the door, and stamped off towards the trees, ignoring the voice from the kitchen window.

'Sam?' the voice called. 'Sammy?' Then, more loudly, '*Samantha*!'

Sam plunged in among the trees, which seemed to hold out leafy arms in welcome. After a moment she glanced back, to find that she could no longer see the cottage through the greenery. Which was just fine, she thought, as she moved deeper into the forest.

She was a slim girl of ten and three-quarters, with short fair hair and a pleasant freckled face. But just then her face was clenched into a furious, thin-lipped scowl.

It had happened again. Just as it had the day

before – the first day of their holiday.

On arrival, Sam had been thrilled by the bright little cottage, the clear blue water of the lake near-by, the vast, silent forest all around. But she had been far from thrilled when her father and her older brother Donald took the boat out 'for a spin' on the lake, leaving Sam and her mother to get the cottage organized.

Being left behind then had made Sam angry enough. But now, on the *second* day of the holiday, her father and brother were going fishing. And Sam was expected to stay with her mother, to do some baking.

Marching on through the forest, Sam snorted at the thought. Just because Donald was two years older and a *boy*, he could go boating and fishing and everything. While she had to stay home and *bake*.

She had been even more enraged by what her father had said. 'You know your mum doesn't like boats, Sammy,' he had told her. 'You two can get on with girl-things, while we men have our adventure.'

That was when Sam had stormed off into the forest. Because if there were adventures to be had, she did *not* want to be left out.

'So I'll have my *own* adventure,' she said aloud to the trees. 'Out here. By myself.'

She peered around, wondering what sort of

102

adventures the forest might offer. The trees didn't grow very big, she saw, but they were close together so that very little sunlight reached the ground. That made a shadowy dimness around Sam, which was slightly spooky. And it was even dimmer amid the riot of ferns and briars and other low plants that sprouted among the trees – or in the many dips and hollows, where narrow ridges of rock showed like teeth through the thin soil.

Sam's father had said that the wilderness went on just like that – trees and brush and rock and all – for hundreds of miles northward from the Great Lakes, where their cottage was. The thought of such a wild vastness around her made Sam slightly uneasy, as she continued on. And so did another thought – about the wildlife.

Most of the forest creatures were fairly harmless, she knew. But her father had said there were supposed to be bears around the lakes. And there might also be wolves.

She had been assured that such beasts stayed well away from places where humans lived. Even so, she did *not* want an adventure that had dangerous animals in it.

Those thoughts were beginning to make the forest seem a little less welcoming. So was the fact that clouds had hidden the sun, making the shadows deeper around her. There was also a heaviness in the air, the warmth of the day seeming more humid in

103

the forest depths. Though she wore only a T-shirt and shorts, Sam was growing quite sweaty as she went on. And no breath of breeze ruffled the trees and bushes around her.

But there *should* be a breeze, she thought sourly. From the fanning wings of all the mosquitoes who saw her as breakfast.

Still, she tried not to let them bother her – just as she tried to ignore the soggy heat, the prickles jabbing her legs, the sharp rock under her tennis shoes. She strode on determinedly, peering around through the veiling leaves, hoping to come upon something exciting or interesting.

Some while later, she was rewarded. The woods presented her with a wonderful clearing, a glade fit for a fairy-tale. Small bright birds flitted and sang overhead; grasshoppers buzzed in the turf; bees and butterflies and dragonflies swarmed among wildflowers.

Sam gazed around, smiling, all anger and uneasiness driven away by the delight of discovery and the beauty of the glade. It would be her own secret place, she thought – her hideaway. And she was choosing a spot where she might make a hidden nest for herself in some tall grass, when a chill breeze swept over the glade and made her shiver.

In fact, it was more of a *wind*, she realized. The

treetops were waving furiously – and above them, huge black clouds swirled and rolled. Even worse, as she looked up, there was a faint muffled rumble of thunder.

Of course, she wasn't *afraid* of thunderstorms. But being outside in a storm, in the heart of a strange wilderness, was different from watching a storm while safe and snug indoors.

I should go back, she thought, and turned to head into the forest again. She moved as quickly as the tangled, rocky ground allowed, while the shadows deepened around her and the growls of thunder grew closer and louder. Then she stumbled and nearly fell as the ground dipped down into a shallow ditch, half-hidden by ferns.

Across the ditch she saw two tall birch trees, ghostly white in the dimness, that had leaned towards each other so that their top branches had become entangled. They made an inverted V, like a pointed arch.

Sam hadn't seen those joined, arching trees before. Nor had she crossed any ditches.

She was going the wrong way.

Staring around at the twilit greenery, she shivered again from a chill that had nothing to do with the wind, while her insides slowly turned shaky and hollow.

The forest looked the same, in every direction.

She had no idea at all which was the *right* way.

She tried to remember her route, but she couldn't recall a thing that she had seen along the way — no special trees or rocks, nothing that would have marked her path. And her heart began thumping in her chest with the breath-stopping shock of knowing that she was lost.

Then another shock made her jump, with a half-shriek. The forest gloom went blindingly bright as an enormous flash of lightning filled the sky. A few seconds later, a monstrous crash of thunder exploded, so loud it almost drove Sam to her knees.

She stumbled away, back towards the clearing, hoping that by starting again from there she might find her way. More spears of lightning scorched across the sky; more bellows of thunder followed. Again and again, blazing and blasting, the fury of the storm fell on the forest, so that Sam began to feel dazed and battered.

She also seemed to be taking a long time to reach the clearing. But then she pushed past a clump of brush and stopped with a gasp. Ahead, she saw two birches leaning together to make a pointed arch, above a shallow ditch.

She had walked in a circle. She couldn't even find the way back to the clearing, let alone the way home.

Fright made her knees feel like cold jelly. Goose bumps rose on her skin as the chill wind moaned through the trees and the lightning shed its pitiless glare. She thought of something her father had said – how in that wilderness people had got lost and were never seen again.

Once more she flinched as the thunder roared, as a new burst of lightning filled the sky. Then, in the pause before the next blast, she went still and pale as if she had turned to marble.

Because in the distance she heard another sound, far more terrifying than thunder.

A howling.

Wolves, she thought. She began to tremble, desperate to run, but not sure which *way* to run, for the wind and the storm made it hard to tell where the howling was coming from. Then the clouds opened, and the first huge drops of rain fell on her like icy arrows.

The cold wetness jolted her into action, a wobbling half-run. As she ran she heard the howling again, seeming to echo among the trees as if she was surrounded.

Panic filled her, driving out all thought, while above her the storm grew even more fierce. Vast lances of lightning struck down at the trees or lashed from cloud to cloud, while the thunder boomed like a million giant cannons and the rain streamed down in almost solid sheets. Half-blinded, half-deafened, half-drowned, Sam staggered on, driven by terror, unsure if the howling she could hear was behind her or ahead.

But suddenly the ground fell away under her feet. Screaming, she plunged down a fern-covered slope, where knuckles of rock bruised her knees and scraped her elbows. Finally she came to a stop, sprawled in mud and soggy leaves, tears of pain and fright filling her eyes. She began to sob, feeling unable to move.

But then she stopped, holding her breath. Something very close by was making almost the same sound, like crying.

A new assault of thunder and lightning showed that she was in a depression like a wide pit. And across the pit, in the lightning's flare, she glimpsed a four-legged shape, a feathery tail, a yellow glint as the light reflected from a pair of eyes.

A wolf, she thought, and might have screamed again except that no sound would come from her mouth. Frantically, she scrambled to her feet – and in the second's lull between thunder-blasts she heard the sound again. Not a wolf-howl or growl. Just a small whimper, a whine.

Lightning ignited the sky once more, and she saw the shape clearly. A smallish shape, with yellow fur and floppy ears and big paws and soft eyes – and a collar. A dog.

Relief swept away Sam's panic and terror. She went towards the dog, which yelped and wagged its tail wildly. It looked like a golden retriever, her favourite kind. Quite a young one, too. Young and lost, like me, Sam thought.

But at least, with a friendly dog, she would no longer be *alone* and lost. And maybe, she thought, she and the dog together could find their way home.

As she drew closer, the dog grew even more excited, its tail thrashing. Yet, oddly, it did not come to her. And in the next blaze of lightning Sam saw why. One of its paws was caught in something.

She knelt by the dog, which wriggled and licked her face. It was a *wire*, she saw, around the left forepaw, its other end fixed to a tree-root. Like some kind of snare that would be used to trap rabbits and other small creatures.

'Poor thing,' she said, stroking the dog's wet fur. 'No wonder you were howling.'

Around her the storm continued its mighty war in the sky, but Sam's attention was wholly on the dog. The lightning helped her as she bent over the wire. It was hard, trying to loosen the snare with only her fingers, and her task was made harder by the dog licking her hands as she worked. But she kept at it, twisting and wiggling the wire – until at last its grip came loose and slid off the paw.

She expected the dog to be even more excited and happy when he was freed. But he jumped up and away from her, up the side of the pit. There he paused, stiff-legged and wild-eyed, hair lifting along his back. Then he simply fled, at top speed, vanishing into the brush.

'You're welcome, I'm sure,' Sam muttered sourly. She felt upset all over again, because she had really wanted the dog's company, and maybe his help. Still, he was a very young dog. And, she thought, if she went in the same direction he had gone, she might find her way.

As she struggled up the side of the pit, the storm seemed to be dying down a little, with longer moments between lightning and thunder. She looked around to see if the dog was in sight, and found that beyond the pit the forest opened out into a broad area where, strangely, no brush or anything at all grew in among the trees. When lightning lit up the gloom, she found that she could see for quite a long way among the slim trunks.

And what she saw, on the far side of that broad open area, turned her again into a white-faced statue, frozen with terror.

She saw a dark, hulking shape on four huge paws, long thick fur flattened by the rain.

A black bear, staring at her.

Sam was so frightened she could barely breathe. She seemed no longer able to hear or feel anything – not the roaring thunder or the chill rain. It was as if she was standing at one end of a long, eerie tunnel, where nothing moved or made a sound, where time itself had stopped.

And at the other end of the tunnel stood the bear, watching her.

In that timeless terrified silence, Sam remained frozen, waiting for the bear to attack. Yet without knowing it, she was doing exactly the right thing. Because terror was keeping her still, she was doing nothing to annoy or alarm the bear, or even to interest it.

Finally, the moment ended. The bear gave a snorting grunt, swung its great head around and lumbered away into the forest depths.

It was another age-long moment before Sam could make herself move. Feeling weak and shaky, she sagged back to lean against the sodden bark of a tree. I'm never going to get out of here, she thought hopelessly. I'm going to wander around, lost, till I starve – or till a wolf or a bear gets me.

Then she jerked upright with a shriek, as something firm and wet and icy-cold jabbed into the back of her bare leg.

Whirling, she saw the young dog – wagging his tail, looking happy all over again now that the bear was gone. Sam knelt to hug his furry neck while he

111

eagerly licked her face. And then she saw a word written on the dog's collar. LUCKY.

'Lucky?' she said, getting to her feet. The dog barked, jumping up at her. 'If that's your name, it suits you.'

She grasped his collar to hold him still – and an idea came to her. Pulling Lucky along, she slid back into the pit, where she wriggled the wire snare free from its fastening. Then she twisted one end of it around Lucky's collar, to make a crude lead.

'Now you'll stay with me,' she told the dog, clutching the wire as they climbed back out. 'Whatever happens.'

By then the storm had faded away almost entirely, save for a few last distant grumbles of thunder. Sam paused on the edge of the pit, trying to decide which way to go. But Lucky was tugging at the wire lead – and when she went forward the dog pulled her along at a brisk pace, in a nearly straight line through the forest, pausing now and then to sniff at a rock or fallen log.

It's as if he's following a scent, despite all the rain, Sam thought. Maybe his own scent, his trail. Maybe he's . . . going home.

No more than twenty minutes later, Sam followed Lucky through a cluster of fir trees – to find that the forest came to a shockingly sudden end. She saw a broad clear area, with a gravel road running up to a cosy cottage. And in its doorway

112

stood a grey-haired woman, looking totally amazed to see the girl and the dog.

Lucky began barking, wagging his tail so hard that he nearly bent double. Then he jerked the wire from Sam's hand and ran to the woman, jumping up at her joyously. She laughed and petted him, calling him by name, then looked curiously again at Sam.

'I . . . found him in the forest,' Sam said shakily. 'I . . . I was lost.'

The woman's eyes went wide. 'Oh, child,' she said in a gentle voice. 'You must have been so frightened. Come in, come in.'

Inside, the woman – who said her name was Mrs West – fetched a towel and a soft robe for Sam to snuggle in while her clothes dried. Then, while Mrs West fed Lucky and gave Sam lemonade and cookies, Sam told the story of her day. Which made Mrs West even more wide-eyed and amazed.

'Samantha, what an adventure!' she said. 'Meeting a *bear* – and rescuing my Lucky . . .'

'He rescued me, too,' Sam said fair-mindedly, 'bringing me out of the forest.' She frowned. 'Though I don't really know where I *am*.'

Mrs West smiled. 'I do,' she said. 'And I'm sure I know where your place is. We can jump in the car and be there in a minute.'

As Sam smiled back, with relief, the clouds outside shifted and a comforting beam of warm sunlight reached in through the window.

'Your parents will have been *very* worried about you,' Mrs West added, 'with that terrible storm and everything. Next time, Samantha, you might be better off staying home with your mother.'

Sam frowned again as she went to put on her dry clothes. Stay *home*, next time? No way, she thought firmly.

Next time, they'd better take me fishing.

REMEMBER MY NAME

by Brian Morse

David mooched on the patio at the back of the villa his family had rented for their month's holiday in Italy. It was three o'clock and stifling hot. Except for him, the world had gone to sleep. Inside, his parents would be dozing on the top of their bed, their holiday paperbacks fallen from their hands, their shutters drawn against the afternoon sun. In the garden nothing moved, not even the leaves of the trees or the few faint wisps of cloud in the sky. The two cats that came with the villa slept in the shade of a wall. A lizard on a rock in the dried-up rockery hadn't shifted a millimetre since that morning. Without moving its eye, it still managed to watch him.

Eventually the sun got too hot for even his

obstinate mood. David moved across the patio, swung his legs over the wall and paddled his sandalled feet in the fractionally cooler air on the other side. Bored with this he jumped off, thinking he'd go down through the wood to the road – one day last week there'd been a donkey standing absolutely still and ownerless in the middle of it – when he chanced to look up the hillside. Something white, high up among the trees, caught his attention. A sheet of newspaper? A piece of cloth? He couldn't imagine what it was. He began to climb towards it.

He was ten metres away when he realized what he was looking at. Under the trees, a girl (she was a woman really, about twenty he guessed) was lying on her side in a blue check-patterned dress, asleep. The white was cloth, a thick piece thrown over her legs. David turned to retreat, embarrassed at having sneaked up on her, when something about the uncomfortable angle at which she was lying, struck him. He edged further up. He noticed more. There was a dark stain on the blanket down by her ankles. Under the blanket there seemed to be something wrong with one of her legs. And suddenly – it made him gasp – he realized what the stain on the blanket was. It was blood.

The moment he gasped, the girl's eyes opened wide. He began to back away, but a slight movement of the gun the girl was pointing at him told him to stay where he was; that this was no game, and that if he made the slightest move there'd be no mercy. She'd shoot him.

The girl looked down past David towards the villa. Involuntarily, David glanced too. Not even the roof was visible from here. He looked back at the girl. The gun was still pointed at him, at his chest. Her finger tightened on the trigger. '*Tu. Sei da solo?*' David didn't understand. If he had, he couldn't have answered. There was a tightness in his chest that threatened to explode.

The girl spoke several sentences to him, very fast. He didn't recognize a single word. More Italian, this time much, much slower. 'English,' he said. '*Inglese,*' at last able to speak. He began to point to himself to make the point absolutely clear, but the squat black gun stopped him.

'*Inglese? Sei inglese!*' The girl seemed disappointed. With a heave she sat up, and David saw the movement hurt her so intensely that for a moment she had to close her eyes. She bit her bottom lip, as if she was preventing herself from crying out. The gun wavered. It was the moment to run from the nightmare, but he couldn't move. His legs were like jelly. Then the girl's eyes re-opened and the gun was pointing at his chest again.

The cloth had slipped off. Her left leg, which she was holding very stiff and unnaturally straight,

119

was stained from her knee to ankle. There was another bandage wrapped round the calf, clotted with blood. David felt sick just to think what it might hide. With an effort the girl focused on him, then looked down at the gun. She hesitated, then lowered it and put it on the ground beside her, hesitated again, then pushed it behind her out of sight. When she smiled, David knew what she was doing. He recognized it from the school playground. It was the bully's trick – a bully who's gone too far; it was an invitation into a conspiracy, the pretence the victim hasn't seen what he has – that she hadn't threatened him. At the very least, that it had all been a mistake.

Trying not to meet her eyes, David stared at where she'd hidden the gun. By the time she got hold of it I'd be halfway down the bank, he thought. It's so unlikely she'd hit me among the trees and the shadows, I'd have nothing to worry about. With that leg she couldn't follow me. I'd be running to fetch the police before she'd got to her feet. But then he remembered his parents, half-asleep, half-awake up in their bedroom. They'd be helpless against her. If I went for help, even with her leg she could probably reach Mum and Dad before the police got here, he reasoned.

As if she knew all this was going through his mind, the girl smiled at him again. 'Trust me,' she was saying. 'Then you'll be safe.' Did he have a choice? David didn't think he had. The girl felt behind her, reassuring herself the gun was still there.

If I'd run, David thought, I wouldn't have got more than a few metres.

'Francesca,' the girl said, tapping her arm.

'David,' he said reluctantly.

'*Tu*,' the girl said, pointing to him. '*Casa*?' She pointed down towards the invisible villa. David nodded, then wished he hadn't. There was a villa at the top of the bank too. He could have pretended he came from there. '*Mamma*? *Papà*?'

'Mum and Dad? Sleeping.' He mimed.

'*Tre*?' The girl put up three fingers. David nodded. Yes, three in the family. 'Please.' she said the word in English. 'Please, *Acqua*.' She mimed drinking. She mimed washing the wound on her leg. She pointed to the house and mimed a picture of David going down and fetching water. Last of all, she pointed to her leg again. '*Mafia*,' she said. '*Capisci*?' She mimed shooting. '*Mafia! Poof!*' She made a gun-banging sound. 'Bad man.' She shrugged.

In the cool of the stone-flagged kitchen, an eye through the window on the point of the patio wall where she'd clamber over if she followed him, David considered. No sound from his parents, so no chance of them catching him filling up

121

the small copper bucket he'd taken from the wall and asking him what on earth he was doing. But plenty of opportunity for him to go upstairs and tell them about her.

He turned off the tap and lifted the bucket out of the sink. It slopped a tablespoonful of liquid. He fetched down a long-handled copper beaker from the wall too. Was he going back or not? He'd have to make up his mind very quickly. How long she'd give him he didn't know, but after a certain point she'd surely decide he'd betrayed her. She'd come down and then there'd be three of them in her power, not just him.

How had she got injured? That was the point. Mafia. He hadn't believed that. But she didn't look criminal – far from it. She looked really respectable. But she had that gun and she'd been prepared to use it. If he'd run when he'd woken her, she'd have shot him. This very moment she might be creeping up on him – on *them*. If she hadn't something to hide, she would ask me to call an ambulance, he thought.

He lifted the bucket, testing its weight, then carried it outside. He let it down with a clatter, but there was no reaction from upstairs. He waited half a minute longer then went back inside. He found a plastic shopping bag and it into put a couple of tea towels from a drawer, the emergency medical kit they kept hanging up by the cooker, then added some bread, some fruit and a half-drunk bottle of wine from the fridge that his father had sealed off with a plastic top.

She was injured. She'd put the gun away. She'd trusted him to come back. She was injured, so whatever she'd done, that put him under a kind of obligation, he told himself wearily. He set off back across the patio and up into the wood.

It was obvious from her look that she hadn't been at all sure he'd return. Nor had she moved a centimetre from where he'd left her. The girl scooped water greedily from the bucket, then tipped out the contents of the bag. She bit into a pear, wolfed down one of the bread rolls, then examined the medical kit. From that she laid aside the Elastoplast, the scissors and a small bottle three-quarters full of liquid.

Now she was turning her attention to her leg. For a sickening moment, David thought she was going to ask him to help, but she didn't. Instead, she bent forward and studied the blood-soaked bandage. She tested its edges. Then she pulled more firmly. 'No!' David said. 'No!' But suddenly she ripped at it. As the bandage came away from her flesh, she screamed. David covered his ears.

In a moment, she'd recovered. Without flinching, she poured the contents of the bottle from the medical kit into the gaping hole of the wound, then cut the towels into two. She fashioned another bandage

123

and Elastoplasted it firmly into place. Then, and only then, she lay back down again. For a moment David thought she'd fainted, but when he touched her arm she looked up at him, her eyes full of tears. Her hand sought his and held it. For a moment he thought about taking the gun – it would have been easy enough – but the idea didn't feel right. He couldn't betray her now, could he? Only as he watched her go to sleep, did he remember how terrified of him she'd been when she'd first woken. Almost as terrified of him as he'd been of her.

'David! David!' His mother's voice came up the hillside. As David tugged his hand free, Francesca woke. Her eyes were as wild as when he'd first surprised her. '*Mamma!*' he whispered fiercely, pointing down towards the villa.

'David! Where are you?' His mother must be by the kitchen door. If she crossed the patio and stepped over into the wood, she'd be sure to look up through the trees and spot them. He could only guess what Francesca's reaction would be if she was seen by an adult.

He pushed off Francesca's hand and started down the bank. Behind him, he heard the girl getting to her feet. He looked over his shoulder as he ran. It was the gun Francesca had been scrabbling for. David slowed to a walk, then stopped altogether. Behind him, he heard the click of the safety catch.

The hair on the back of his neck was bristling. Very carefully, he turned. Francesca had the gun trained two-fisted on him. Suddenly she raised it and aimed somewhere beyond him, at where his mother would appear if she came to the edge of the patio to look up into the trees.

David made a circular movement with his hand to mean, 'I'm returning,' but there was no response from Francesca. 'David!' his mother called once more. Francesca adjusted her aim.

Very carefully, David began walking again, placing each foot so it would make no sound – nothing to attract his mother's attention.

His mother was on the other side of the patio, peering towards the road. 'There you are,' she said. She yawned. 'I slept hours. Your dad's still asleep. Everything all right?'

'Mm.'

His mother looked in the direction he'd come from. David willed her not to move a centimetre that way. If she even went as far as the wall, Francesca would have her properly in her sights. If his mother raised her eyes and saw the gun, what would her reaction be? To scream? Francesca would shoot her. He knew it. 'You don't usually go up there,' his mother said.

'I've a game going.'

'On your own?'

'Of course!'

He must have sounded alarmed at the suggestion. 'I only wondered if you'd met someone to play with,' his mother said. 'That property over the top – someone said they had children.'

'No,' he said. 'Only—'

'Only what?'

It was his chance to say.

'Only – only nothing.' He steadied his voice. Nothing to alarm Francesca, who would be able to hear every word. 'What are you and Dad going to do now?'

'I've a book I want to finish. Later, we'll probably stroll down to the village and have a drink in the café. Your dad's been mugging up on some words he wants to try out. You'll be OK till then?' She looked up into the trees doubtfully. 'You're all right on your own? Not lonely?' She took a step that way. 'Why don't I go up with you, explore a bit, give you some company?'

'I'm fine,' he said. 'Honestly.' He jumped back over the patio wall. 'Anyway, I'll probably go down the road in a minute. To finish off.' Any lie to keep her from setting foot in the wood.

As he climbed towards her, Francesca slowly lowered the gun. The sound of her putting the safety catch on seemed like an explosion in itself.

It was still early, but soon enough the shadows

would begin creeping down the hillside through the trees. His parents (so close on the patio – Dad was there now – he only had to raise his voice to get their attention) would call him to get ready to go out. Whatever Francesca had done, she ought to be in hospital. He had to do something about her. What was she waiting here for? To die? He felt angry with her. Why couldn't she have chosen someone else's wood to hide in?

Francesca beckoned him to lean over her. '*Telefono*,' she said in a whisper. '*Mio amico*. Yes? Friend.' Another English word she'd found.

David nodded. Yes. A solution. But then he thought, How will I know what to say? It was impossible. He could only communicate in English.

'*Telefono*,' Francesca insisted.

Then he realized what they could do. He mimed writing.

'*Bene!*' Francesca said. '*Bene*.'

David got up to fetch paper. 'David!' she said, her voice too loud. She pointed to her leg. '*Mafia*,' she said. '*Capisci?*' Again she mimed shooting. He knew she was lying, but it gave him a way out – an excuse for helping someone he almost certainly shouldn't. He patted her hand. 'It'll be OK,' he said.

'OK,' she echoed him.

Mum and Dad were in deckchairs reading when he climbed over the patio wall. 'Finished whatever you're up to?' Dad said. He glanced at his watch. 'Give it half an hour and I'll be getting peckish. What about you?'

'I'm still playing,' David said. 'Do we have to go so soon?'

David ran as fast as he ever had in his life, past the row of new villas on the outskirts of the village, past the A.G.I.P. garage, past the bread shop, past the yard where the donkey he'd found on the road belonged. He burst into the piazza. It seemed unusually crowded with vehicles, but his mind had room for only one thing – getting to the phone, passing the message on, getting rid of the threat and burden of Francesca. He dodged between two dark blue vehicles and weaved his way through the tables outside Café Borsa, the café the family used. He would get *gettoni*, the tokens for the telephone, from Sebastiano, the barman. He knew what to say. He'd done it before. There was a public telephone tucked away in the corner of the bar and they used it to phone his grandparents every three or four days.

In his haste, he brushed against a customer's arm and heard the tinkle of a cup overturning in a saucer. There was a curse. David stopped, afraid of having drawn attention to himself, embarrassed at having been so clumsy. He hopped round to apologize as best he could and the guilt rose into his face. The

129

man whose arm he'd banged was a policeman. The other men at the table were policemen too. Suddenly he saw the two blue cars he'd run between had *CARABINIERI* painted in tall letters down their sides. There were other policemen in the square as well. In the far corner, a battered-looking green car had been roped off with white tape. Watched by a group of village children, two men were examining it. David knew whose car it was.

The policeman banged the cup straight and shouted. David stood absolutely still. The policeman, an officer glistening with stripes and buttons, stood up. '*Cretino!*' he shouted. David understood that much! But his eyes strayed to the battered green car. There was a stain on the passenger seat which the plainclothesman was carefully examining. He stared. Francesca's blood? Or was he imagining it?

The officer, red-faced with anger, shouted again, then someone put an arm round David's shoulders and held him in a vice-like grip. He began to struggle, but whoever was holding him blew in his ear. '*Il nostro piccolo inglese!*' Our little Englishman! It was the barman, Sebastiano.

Our little Englishman – that seemed to amuse the policeman. He laughed and sat down. He said something under his breath and nodded in David's direction. The table erupted with laughter. Sebastiano released David and tidied round the table. He winked at David. 'Make yourself scarce,' his look said. *Il nostro piccolo inglese.*

For a moment David hated them all, even Sebastiano. He ran on into the bar and leant against the counter until Sebastiano came back in, balancing cups and saucers on his tray. David thrust the bank note Francesca had given him across the counter. '*Gettoni, per piacere.*'

'*Tanti?*' Sebastiano said, and David suddenly realized how much the note was worth – more than twenty English pounds. He quickly held up all ten fingers. Surely that would be enough? '*Va bene.*' Sebastiano came back from the cash register with the *gettoni*, a wad of notes and half a dozen coins.

'*Grazie.*' David stowed the money away in his pocket.

Sebastiano pointed to the policemen outside. '*Macchina*,' he said and made pretence of driving a car. He banged a gun. 'Bad woman – *terrorista*,' he said. He held two fingers to his head and fired. He held the fingers up. 'Three dead.' He sighed. 'Bad woman.' He touched David on the arm. 'You – home – quick!'

David walked to the phone at the far end of the bar. He was trembling. He felt frightened – not of danger, but of not doing his duty. He took the paper with its message for Francesca's friend out of his pocket. Mafia! Of course he'd known that was rubbish all along, but now Sebastiano had spelt it

131

out – Francesca was a murderess.

'Phoning England?' Very slowly, David turned.

It wasn't Sebastiano but one of the policemen from the table outside. David had noticed him because he hadn't seemed as amused at the officer's joke as the others. The policeman inclined his head to look at the paper in David's hand.

David looked away. No use pretending it was an English telephone number. It didn't have enough digits. He shook his head. 'I'm phoning someone here,' he said. 'Someone who—'

'Know how to use Italian phones?' The man's accent was American.

'Mm.'

'Got it all written down what to say? Or do they speak English?' As if he knew what David was doing – almost as if he was teasing him – the policeman was staring even more closely at the piece of paper on the back of which David had written down what Francesca wanted him to say as it had sounded to him. 'I worked in New York three years,' the policeman said. 'That's how come I speak English. Sure you don't want help?' He extended his hand for the paper. 'My boss—' He nodded his head towards the table outside. 'He's—' He didn't say more, but gently tugged the paper from David's hand.

David looked up into the adult's face. With relief he realized there was no way the policeman could ring the number and read out the message without realizing what was going on. It was the right thing to happen, wasn't it? Francesca ought to be caught, oughtn't she? I was scared she would shoot my mum and dad. She threatened me. The excuses would come easily. No-one would disbelieve him.

'A Ravenna number. Not so very far away.' The policeman took a couple of *gettoni* and put them in the slot. He lifted the receiver and began to dial. 'You going to speak, or me?' He flipped the paper over and glanced at the back of it.

Or David could run and reach Francesca before they did – help her get further into the woods . . . He remembered how badly she was injured, how pretty she was, how gentle she'd been with him after she'd come to trust him, how bravely she'd faced her pain, how she'd come to depend on him . . .

'Pongiluppi! Pongiluppi!' An angry voice called into the bar. The policeman jumped.

'Listen,' David said. 'Please—'

'Sorry,' the policeman said. 'My boss. I got to go. The people you're phoning – they're answering. You'll have to manage.'

David went up into the trees next morning, the first time since he and Francesca had rehearsed the message, whatever it had been. Of course Francesca wasn't there; there was no sign she ever had been. The half-empty bottle of wine had gone – everything, even the core of the pear, had disappeared.

The family drove into Ravenna late in the morning. After lunch in a restaurant, Dad spread out on the table the newspaper he'd picked up at the village kiosk. With a sigh he consulted his dictionary.

'Who's that on the front?' Mum asked. 'She looks pretty. An actress, is she? Or a beauty queen?'

Dad looked. So did David.

'It's Anna-Maria Beraducci,' Dad said after a moment. 'A terrorist they're looking for.'

'Her? She's so pretty.' Mum said, horrified. 'What did she do?'

Dad read through the article. 'There's a few words I'm not sure of,' he said eventually, 'but she seems to have been part of a gang that tried to kidnap a politician yesterday. There was a shoot-out. One of the gang was killed, and two of the politician's guards. They think this woman was injured.' He read some more then said excitedly, 'They found her car in our village! Would you believe it! It had been abandoned in the village square. They've no idea how she got away unless someone in the village helped her. They got her companion but not her. If David hadn't felt ill last night we would have gone down for a drink and seen all that!'

The postcard came just before they left for home, postmarked Milan – the only post they got the whole time they were at the villa. It was addressed to *il giovane inglese* – the young Englishman. *Grazie, Francesca* was all it said. Someone whose dog he'd helped to find, David told his parents. He'd forgotten to tell them about it.

He put up with Dad's teasing about beautiful *signorinas* for the morning, then tore up the card when no-one was looking. He'd broken the law for her – for a kidnapper, a murderess. He threw the pieces of the card in the bin. She could at least have trusted him with her name. She could at least have remembered his.

HUMAN SHIELD

by Anthony Masters

The man was standing in the middle of the dusty suburban road, his arms outstretched, while another stood on the pavement, a rifle in his hands. Overhead, the sun was already high in the Kuwaiti sky, and even at eight o'clock in the morning the heat was intense.

'Here we go again,' said the driver. 'More Iraqi checks.'

Everyone groaned. The bus, full of English and American pupils bound for the International School in Kuwait City, had frequently been stopped ever since Kuwait had been invaded by Iraq. There was usually a long delay while papers were inspected, but not more than that. Ten-year-old Will Harper wasn't afraid – not for himself at least, but he was

137

continuously afraid for his father who had been taken from their home over a week ago.

Brian Harper had been forced to join many of his colleagues across the border in one of the Iraqi aircraft factories. Horrifyingly, it was rumoured that they might be used as a human shield against the Allied bombing of key Iraqi sites, and his plight never left Will's mind. His mother had remained very strong, reassuring him and his little sister, but even her calm exterior did nothing to ease Will's anxiety – mainly because he knew that his father was already in a very fragile mental state. Because he was an engineer working for the Kuwaitis on a new fighter aircraft, he had not only been roughly questioned by the Iraqis but had already been kept for a week in a windowless room before being returned home. He had only been back with them for a few days before he was seized again.

Will looked up towards the front of the school bus. All the linguistic schools had been closed, but the International School had been allowed to keep going so that the Iraqi invaders could keep tabs on the movements of European teachers, parents and pupils. The driver was arguing with an Iraqi soldier who was holding up a list, and Will could see that more of the militia had gathered outside. All of them were holding weapons and there seemed to be an air of serious menace this morning. Suddenly

Will realized that this was much more than a regular check.

Seconds later, Will's name was called. His was the only one and he stood up automatically, as if he had been at school. The other pupils stared at him as he walked dazedly up the length of the bus. Why should he be called? It must be something to do with his father. Please God, he thought suddenly, don't let him have cracked up. Or worse.

'William Harper?' The Iraqi soldier was still studying his list.

'Yes.'

'You come with me.'

'You can't do that,' said the driver. 'I've got to take him to school.'

'No school.'

'Why?' The driver was in his sixties, an old-style Empire kind of Englishman, now retired and trying to be useful. Will knew that he didn't stand nonsense from anyone, but he hoped he wasn't going to argue with the soldier. Will knew all too well how that would end.

The soldier ignored the question and turned to Will. 'You are going to join your father.'

He didn't know what to say. 'Why?' he asked after a slight hesitation.

'Your father make much trouble. If you come, things will be easier.'

'Will they?'

'Yes.' The soldier nodded confidently.

'I told you,' interrupted the elderly driver. 'The boy isn't going anywhere. He's in my charge.'

'He's coming with me. Stop arguing.' The soldier's voice had an edge to it, but the driver wasn't giving in. He stood in the doorway and folded his arms across his chest. The pupils watched him in deadly fascination.

'Get out of the way.' The soldier gave him one last chance. More militiamen outside were already closing in, their guns upraised and their expressions ranging from contemptuous amusement to anger. Then the soldier raised his hand and hit the driver round the face, and another soldier seized his arm, hauling him off the bus.

Will tried to follow him down the steps, but the Iraqi grabbed him round the neck. 'Leave him,' Will yelled. 'I'll come with you, but don't hurt him any more. Please.'

Will was bundled into a jeep with a different soldier at the wheel and two more sitting on either side of him in the back.

'Where are we going?' asked Will, but neither of the soldiers spoke as the vehicle hurtled along, blaring its harsh and discordant horn at a straggling herd of goats and their panicky goatherd. They were beyond the suburbs now, out in the desert with dunes beginning to stretch on either side of them – hundreds of miles of unblemished sand. The road ran straight as a die, and fairly regularly they passed Iraqi tanks and personnel carriers that poured along the two-lane highway in a steady and relentless stream.

Once, one of the soldiers passed him a flask of cold water which Will sipped at gratefully, and later another gave him a little rice cake. He still wasn't exactly afraid but deeply concerned about his father, who was gentle and rather vague, often so absorbed by his work that he hardly knew what was going on around him. Will loved him dearly and was wondering how he was managing without them. The family had become very close and self-sufficient as they travelled the world in the course of his father's work. Will knew that his father was a brave man – he had been in some of the world's biggest trouble spots during the course of his long career – but he also suffered very badly from claustrophobia. The windowless room had almost broken him, so what would more imprisonment do to him? Will was also worried about his mother, and tears filled his eyes when he pictured her being told about what had happened to him. Both soldiers noticed the dampness on his cheeks and the older of the two put his arm round Will and roughly squeezed his shoulder.

'No worry.'

'What will my mother say?'

'Mother be told. Mother be happy.'

'How is my father?' But his captors didn't reply and soon an airfield came into view, with low-lying hangars and some factory buildings. The jeep pulled up at a security gate, which was quickly raised, and they drove into a compound of temporary-looking huts which had been put up just in front of the factory buildings. The soldiers motioned Will to get out. They then escorted him into one of the larger huts, through a reception area and into a large office where they stood quickly to attention, shouldering their rifles as they did so.

Behind a desk was a large Iraqi officer with a moustache. He looked so familiar that Will involuntarily gasped.

'You Saddam Hussein?' he said in amazement.

The man roared with laughter, came over and clapped Will on the shoulder. 'You make a good joke,' he said in English. 'Many people think that I have a likeness to His Excellency and now you.' He paused. 'Are you a clever boy?'

'Just average, I suppose,' Will replied guardedly.

'Your father is sick. He shoots his mouth off. All day and all night.'

'If he's sick, why don't you let him go?' said

142

Will truculently, but inside he felt deeply afraid.

'And there's something else,' added the officer.

Could there be anything else? wondered Will.

'Your father – he has plans to escape. You tell him – if he tries, you will both be shot.' Instinctively Will knew that this was not the time to answer back.

'Your father is an important man and it is imperative I keep him here,' the officer continued.

'As a hostage?' asked Will, but he didn't answer directly.

'I am very worried. You must talk to him – make sure he calms down.'

Will shook his head. 'You've made him ill – I can't help you.'

'You must,' was the implacable reply.

His escorts took Will away from the office, back into the jeep, and then drove across the airfield into another compound with factory buildings and more huts. But this time there was a high chain-wire fence, spotlights and a watch-tower. The jeep stopped at an outer fence and Will was pushed towards a young guard, almost a boy, who took him inside. For a moment, Will thought he heard one of his former captors say, 'Good luck,' but he wasn't quite sure and he didn't have time to think much about it as he was pushed into a long, low concrete hut and the door was slammed hard behind him.

143

'Dad!' His father looked much worse than he had done when he had returned from the interrogation. There was a hunted feel to him, and he hesitantly pulled at the buttons on his shirt. When he saw Will, he went ashen and slowly raised trembling, outstretched arms.

'What the hell are you doing here?'

Will flew to him and, as they embraced, Brian Harper began to shake. Sitting on the edge of his father's bed, Will glanced around the large dormitory. There were a couple of dozen men in there. They were all civilians; some of them European and others Kuwaiti. He caught sight of one Kuwaiti boy of about his own age, but his attention was almost instantly drawn back to his father who had his head in his hands and was rocking himself to and fro. He was not in tears as Will had first thought, but in a rage of frustration. When he had finished cursing the Iraqis for the way they had used their prisoners as human shields, he went on to condemn them for abducting Will. 'They're animals,' he said. 'The Allies bomb this area most nights, and they've scored a couple of direct hits on the other side of the airfield. To bring a child here – it's monstrous!'

'There's one here already,' said Will, pointing to the Kuwaiti boy.

'That's Sami. He's Ghazi's son. They were brought in together because his housekeeper walked out and there was no-one to care for him.'

'So if he can be here, so can I.'

'They've done it to get back at me,' said his father angrily.

'What have you been doing, Dad?' asked Will cautiously.

'I suppose you could say I've been heading up the escape committee.'

'So I heard.' What was he going to do? wondered Will. Should he tell his father they would both be shot if any escape attempt was made? He could see how mentally sick his father was, but how could he help him? There was an odd, glittering look in his eyes and the sweat stood out on his forehead. Will wondered how near his father was to a total breakdown.

Then the door was thrown open again and the man who looked like Saddam Hussein walked in, flanked by the guards.

'That's Tareq al-Hakim,' whispered Will's father. 'He's the Commanding Officer here.'

'Gentlemen.' Al-Hakim looked round appraisingly at the assembled company. 'Gentlemen – and two boys.' He laughed at his tiny joke, but his laughter was automatic and there was something in al-Hakim's eyes that Will couldn't place. Then, with a shock, he understood. The man was afraid.

'There is a new development.'

Will felt a tremor of apprehension.

'Bad news, I'm afraid.'

Will looked at his father and saw that he was staring intently up at al-Hakim.

'As you know, we have so far treated you very humanely – with great decency.' There was a long, uneasy pause. 'Each time the bombers have come, we have taken you to a shelter.'

'A very inadequate shelter,' muttered someone.

Al-Hakim's eyes rested on the man who had spoken. Strangely, they were full of compassion. 'Nevertheless, it was shelter. Now I'm afraid I can't even give you that.'

This time it was Ghazi who spoke up. He looked very young – too young to be a father, thought Will, with his slight frame and dark wavy hair. He looked like Sami's older brother, not his father. 'What do you mean by that?'

'I mean that we have repeatedly told your people, particularly the aggressors – the Americans – that we will use you as a human shield. But they don't take us seriously and have bombed us continuously. They show us contempt.' Al-Hakim's voice shook. 'We have warned them not to come tonight. His Excellency, our own Saddam Hussein, has warned them. But they won't listen.'

The chill crept over Will's body.

'So they must learn their lesson.'

'What are you saying?' asked Ghazi apprehensively.

'Tonight you will not go to the shelter. You will stay here. You will be our shield – for the first time. The Americans have been told, so it is up to them. Entirely up to them.'

'We wouldn't stand a chance,' said Brian Harper.

'We must hope they withdraw. If not, Mr Bush will be more of a murderer than we thought he was.'

'No,' said Ghazi quietly. 'It's you who are that.'

'You can't do this.'

'We don't stand a chance.'

'We're a sitting target.'

All the men were shouting at al-Hakim now, but Will knew that the officer wasn't listening – that he had closed his mind to them.

'Let us pray they will change their minds – that the raid will not take place.'

There was a long, impenetrable silence.

'You must realize,' said al-Hakim at last, 'that we mean business. You will be locked in, and if you are foolish enough to try and escape – either now or if your bombers come – you will be shot.'

He walked quickly out of the room, the guards close behind him, and the door was shut, bolted and barred. Will watched the sweat intensify on his father's forehead and saw a little pulse beat in his cheek, and his heart sank. He remembered how he had once been in a broken-down train with his father and how he had seen similar signs of panic in his face. On that occasion Will had talked to him, trying desperately to reassure him, for he was terrified his father would simply jump out and land on the live rail. Fortunately, the train had moved off. But here, in this smelly, closed-in room, there was nowhere to go, no chance of rescue. How could he calm his father here? Will felt a great weight of crushing responsibility, but he knew he had to see his father through this somehow. Then a tiny spark of hope glowed in his mind. After all – the windowless room hadn't broken him completely. Was there a chance that Brian Harper could keep control?

Ghazi was on his feet, stacking chairs and beds in the centre of the room and looking at his watch at the same time. 'Come on, Brian.' He was sweating as men rushed up to help him and his son, Sami, pull a table across the room. 'Let's make some barricades.'

Brian Harper shook his head. 'There won't be enough protection.' He stayed broodingly apart.

'What else have we got?' yelled someone.

'The floorboards,' Ghazi snapped. 'Come on, everyone, there's a broken one over there. Let's get 'em up. We've got about an hour before they come – if they're coming.'

'That's right!' yelled someone else. 'They don't always come, do they?'

'Yes, they do,' said Ghazi stolidly. 'They come

148

most nights and I don't think this is going to be an exception.'

Will found that he was tearing up the floorboards with his bare hands, hardly believing what was happening, still consumed with fear – not about the promised air-raid, but how he could deter his father from doing something crazy. Then he realized that Sami was beside him. He was small but very wiry and strong, and seemed to be making much more of an impression on the hard, wooden boards than Will was.

'How long you been here?' asked Will.

'Ten days.'

'Isn't your mum at home?'

'No. She died a long time ago. But I wanted to be here – to be here with my dad.'

Will nodded. It wasn't so simple for him. His father also needed help, but not from the menace of the Americans or even the Iraqis. Will would have to protect him from himself.

'Will.' The summons came that he had been dreading, and he returned to his father's side.

Brian Harper's eyes were still glittering brightly and his hand shook as he grabbed Will's arm.

'I've got us a way out,' he muttered, staring around him in case he was overheard. 'And we're going to take it. When I say run – we dive for the door and then—' He paused. 'And then we head across the yard, dodging the spotlight, keeping

close to the shadows of the buildings.' He paused
again, gripping Will's arm until it hurt.

'What then, Dad?'

'There's a shower block and a warehouse.'

'And?'

'That warehouse backs on to the perimeter wire.'
He was gabbling now, staring ahead with a wild
intensity as if he could smell freedom. 'It's two
storeys high.'

'So?' Will knew the scheme was wild but he
couldn't think how to stop it happening.

'Don't you see – we could jump over the wire.
Dead easy.'

'Dead's the word,' replied Will forcefully. 'Suppose we're too high up?'

'That's the risk we're going to have to take,'
replied his father sharply.

'But we haven't sussed it out,' Will protested.
'And we'll never be able to break open the door.'

'We've just got to take our chances.'

'How can we?'

'Now, are you with me, Will?' His father stared
at him, his eyes wilder than ever. Then he added,
'Look, old son, we don't have any choice. We've
got to go somehow – for your mother's sake.'

Will wavered and then made one last stab at
trying to stop him.

'Suppose she loses us both?'

But Brian Harper wouldn't see reason. 'And that's exactly what's going to happen if we stay here.' He glanced round contemptuously at the men in the hut, working away to protect themselves – trying to erect some all too obviously inadequate defences.

'It's dark now and the American bombers will be here soon. Look at those fools—' His contempt deepened. 'They're all going to die – trapped in here.'

'They've got more of a chance in here than—' began Will, but he was interrupted by harsh bursts of anti-aircraft fire from the compound and the deafening thunder of a fighter jet. He froze – as did everyone else in the hut. Then someone whispered, 'Dear God – here they come.'

'You ready?' asked Brian Harper.

'No – you've got to stay,' whispered Will. 'Dad, you *can't*.'

There was a thumping, rending sound from some distance away. 'That's a hit,' Ghazi said.

'We'll be next,' someone groaned.

Brian sprang for the window. 'Forget the door – this frame's weak,' he muttered, tugging and pulling at the rotten wood until it wrenched open. Then he started to climb through.

'Don't be a fool, Brian!' yelled Ghazi, grabbing at his legs but getting a kick in the face for his efforts.

He reeled back, shouting, 'You'll die out there.' But Brian Harper was gone and, within seconds, Will was following him.

'You can't go out there!' bellowed Sami. 'They'll shoot you— Didn't you hear what they said?'

'I heard,' replied Will feverishly, 'but I've got to be with my dad, haven't I? I've got to help him.'

'He's ill,' shouted Ghazi, but his words were drowned by the roar of another incoming jet.

The night was pitch dark outside and the noise of the anti-aircraft fire and the jets was incredible. For a devastating moment, Will couldn't see his father, but just as the panic was rising from his stomach, he caught a glimpse of him, crouched in the shadows of the next building.

'Dad—'

'Get down, shut up – and run.' The long, hard beam of the searchlight was travelling towards them.

Brian Harper sprinted towards the next building – and Will followed him, the adrenalin surging, but with it a knob of hardening fear in his chest.

They both continued their deadly game with the spotlight for at least two more buildings, whilst the jets howled above them and the bombs seemed to rain down on the factory, which was now on fire.

The crackling of flames, a collapsing roof, an explosion – and then a sulphurous stench was in Will's nostrils as he pursued the darting, lunging shape of his father's determined body through the devastation of the night. Somehow they managed to avoid most of the spotlight's beams, yet Will was certain that his father had plunged through it for a brief but potentially fatal second. Had he been seen, or was the air-raid occupying all of the Iraqis' energy?

They paused, frozen in silhouette by the door of a larger two-storey building. Suddenly his father ducked down and ran inside and up a staircase which seemed to go on for ever. They were standing by a small window through which they could see, in wan moonlight, the desolate landscape of the desert beyond the security fence. A fire in the compound opposite the building lit the interior of the building they were in, and Will could see that they were standing in a large, bare space with some old machinery at one end.

His gaze returned to his father who was standing, staring out, all too well aware that if they jumped they would break their legs, if not their necks.

'It's no good, Dad,' whispered Will. 'There's no way out. Let's get back before we're caught. We can stick it out somehow, the two of us.'

'We're not going back in that hole.' There was a sob in his voice. 'We'll die.'

153

'Yes, you are going back,' said Will sternly. How strange, he thought. It's as if I'm *his* father, not the other way round. Then he heard footsteps coming up the stairs and, as they crunched relentlessly upwards, the sound of the planes and the bombing seemed to grow fainter.

'We've got to hide – someone's coming.'

'We're going through that window,' replied Brian Harper. 'And no-one's stopping us.'

Will knew that his father was desperate enough to try and break out, so he grabbed him round the waist and hung on. Then a voice from the stairs said quietly, 'Please don't move – I have a gun.'

Al-Hakim stood there, a revolver in his hand.

'Stop struggling, Mr Harper, or I'll shoot both of you.'

'We've got to get out—'

'Dad – he'll kill us. You've got to think of Mum – you've got to think of us all.'

His father hesitated.

'Keep away from the window.'

'You'll not keep us here.'

'Unfortunately, we have to.'

Brian Harper smashed the glass with his fist and Will could see the blood running down his wrist. 'Dad,' he yelled as angrily as al-Hakim. 'He'll shoot us. He means what he's saying.'

'I certainly do.' Al-Hakim snapped off the safety catch and took aim, as more glass was smashed.

154

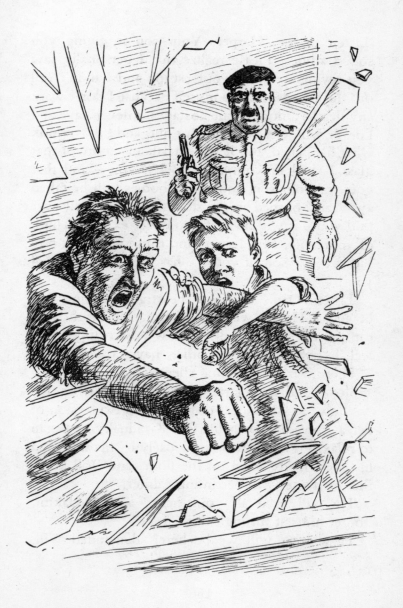

'Listen to me, Harper. Your son is giving you sound advice. Please realize that I personally saw you trying to make your escape and I didn't call out the guards. I came myself because I don't want any deaths amongst our hostages. I never have and I never will. Get back to your hut, and I'll overlook what happened, but if you smash any more of that glass I shall be compelled to kill you – and that goes for your son, too. Your bodies will be taken away and burned in the desert. No-one will ever find you – it will be as if you never existed. Think of your wife, Mr Harper, and think what this boy – this brave son of yours – has been trying to tell you.'

'Listen, Dad.' Will had the strange feeling that he and al-Hakim were in alliance. 'He's right. We can get over to the hut. I know how trapped you feel, but we've got each other, haven't we?'

There was a long, long silence.

Slowly, Brian Harper moved away from the window, his shoulders down and an expression of defeat spreading over his face. Gradually he began to relax, his hands hanging loosely by his sides and his eyes firmly fixed on the floor, and Will knew that his father was becoming calmer.

'He will need all your help,' said al-Hakim, 'to get himself through these days.'

'How long will we be here?' demanded Will,

knowing there would be, could be, no answer. Al-Hakim shrugged. 'There will be the mother of all battles soon, but it will be in the desert, not in the air. On that will depend how long we have to keep you. Come – take him back now. I will come with you to ensure your safety.'

Will held his father's arm as the oddly assorted trio walked back past the factory buildings towards the hut. The night was quieter now. The bombers had flown away and Iraqi fire-fighting crews were dealing with a number of different blazes that were scattered around the compound.

'The hut's not even damaged,' said Will as they drew nearer. 'Can we go in the shelter next time? Nothing's going to stop the Americans, is it?' As he spoke, he felt on an equal level with al-Hakim, as if they were colleagues discussing a tricky situation. It was a weird sensation but al-Hakim must have felt it too, for the Iraqi officer answered almost confidingly, 'I'll talk to our commander. Your presence was clearly not a deterrent.' He lowered his voice. 'I must have your guarantee that your father does not try to escape again.'

'I shall do my best,' said Will, 'but I can't give any guarantee.'

'You came here as a child,' said al-Hakim. 'Now, in a few hours, you have become a man.'

Will nodded. The man was right. The words

rang in his head as they entered the close confines of the hut again. Once inside, Will breathed in the animal smell of fear. It wasn't going to be easy.

A MATTER OF TIME

by Sue Welford

Amita lay motionless, the faraway thunder of the explosion still echoing in her ears. She coughed, choking on the dry, biting dust. Her eyes stung. Something warm and sticky ran down her forehead and over her closed, terrified eyelids.

When at last she opened her eyes, Amita could see nothing. Clouds of pink dust swirled around her like a sandstorm. Tentatively, she raised her head. She moved her arm to wipe away the stickiness from her face. Looking down, she saw it was blood. She lay still, still as death, hardly even daring to breathe.

A few metres away, Jonathan Holroyd struggled to sit up. Dull light from the below-pavement-level window made routes through the swirling dust.

Jonathan could just make out a metal girder rest-
ing against a pile of shattered bricks. The end of
the girder was across his leg. His fingers reached
out and clasped something. When he brought his
hand into view, he saw it was a Barbie doll. Her
silver cocktail dress was torn and tattered. Half her
face was gone. Somewhere in the distance Jonathan
thought he heard a scream.

Carefully, Jonathan tried to withdraw his foot.
Immediately, an agonizing, searing pain shot up his
leg. He yelled. The air seemed to spin and hover in
front of him. Dizzy with pain, he lay back on the
hard, rubble-strewn floor and began to cry. Hot
tears made rivers in the dry dust on his face. He
could hear the insistent drip, drip of water from a
fractured pipe.

'Who is it . . . who's there?'

It sounded like a girl. Jonathan wiped the mois-
ture from his cheeks, feeling the scratchy plaster
score his skin. He sniffed. There was a smell. Something nasty – a metallic kind of smell. Jonathan
sneezed. The dust was beginning to clear now, set-
tling on the ruined basement floor of the department
store. He sat up again. Slowly this time. He took a
deep breath and the world stopped spinning.

Across the fallen beam he could just make out
a figure. It was lying on the ground, covered with
large fragments of plaster.

'It's me!' Jonathan cried. He tried to move but

fell back, pain shrieking up his leg.

The voice came again. Weak but perfectly clear.

'Who's me?'

'Jonathan . . .'

'Where are you, Jonathan? I can't see you.'

'I'm here.'

Jonathan saw the figure move, begin to turn over. As it did so, there was a deep rumble and not far away another beam fell with a crash. Clouds of dust and debris rose like an eruption. A tangle of twisted metal fell from above, bouncing like a crazy, agonized spider.

Jonathan froze. Then he whispered hoarsely, 'I think you'd better stay still.'

The voice came back to him. 'Yes.'

There was silence for a little while. Miles away, Jonathan could hear the scream of sirens and deep rumbles that seemed to come from the bowels of the earth.

A bit later, the girl's voice came again.

'Are you OK, Jonathan?'

'I . . . I think so. My leg's stuck under this beam thing. It . . . it really hurts.' Jonathan felt the tears come again. He brushed them away. If only he hadn't insisted on being 'grown up' and gone down to the basement to get his dad's Christmas present by himself, everything would have been all right. He patted his coat pocket. The present for his dad was still there, safe, not at all squashed. The feel

161

of the small box gave him a sense of reassurance.

He heard the girl again. 'Best not try to move, Jonathan. I'm sure someone will come to rescue us soon.'

'They won't know we're here.'

'Yes they will. Someone will . . .'

'Where are your mum and dad?' Jonathan asked.

'At home. Mum told me not to come shopping. She said they'd threatened a bombing campaign . . .'

'Do you think that's what it was then . . .?'

'I don't know . . . Where are your parents, Jonathan?'

Jonathan sniffed. His leg was going numb now, right up to the top. 'They've gone next door to the Pizza Hut to wait for me. I was just getting my dad's present, then we were going to have dinner.'

'I expect they'll be all right then.'

'Yes . . .'

Jonathan saw the figure shift again, awkwardly, like a puppet that had lost its strings. 'They'll know where you are. They'll tell the rescuers.'

'I hope the rescuers come soon.' Jonathan sniffed again. There was still that funny smell. He'd smelt it before somewhere but couldn't think where.

'They will, Jonathan. They'll be looking already. I know they will.'

'What's your name?' Jonathan called.

162

'Amita.'

'What do you think has happened to the others, Amita?'

'What others?'

'The other people who were looking at the toys and the sports stuff next door. There was a lady with a baby in a pram . . .' Jonathan didn't want to think about it.

There was another small silence. 'I don't know.' Then Amita called, 'Is anyone else there . . .? Anyone else . . . alive?'

Only silence answered. Jonathan couldn't even hear the sirens any more.

'Jonathan?'

'Yes . . .' Jonathan sniffed, crying silently with fear and pain.

'I'm going to try to get over to you.'

'OK . . . No . . . you'd better not.' Jonathan looked up fearfully. Above his head, cables and wires swung precariously. There was a great, jagged hole in the ceiling. Brightly coloured ladies' clothes hung through like ragged washing. It looked as if the whole lot might come down at any minute.

Jonathan heard a kind of scraping sound. He turned his head sideways. Someone who looked like a scarecrow was crawling towards him. The figure pushed away a pile of boxes with spaceships inside, moved gingerly beneath a fallen beam. At last it reached him.

It was the girl, although you'd never have known it. She had pink, dusty hair. It looked as if it had once been woven into a single, thick plait down the back. Blood was running down her face. It made roadways down her cheek and you could see the dark skin beneath the pale dust. One earlobe was torn and bloody, the other held a gold ring. There was a long rent in her tracksuit trousers. Jonathan could see blood there, too.

As she reached him, the girl put out her hand and clutched his. Then she managed a kind of wobbly smile. There was so little room she could hardly even sit up properly. She just lay beside him, clutching on to his hand as if it was a life-line.

After a few minutes, the girl pushed back a lock of hair that had escaped from its plait. She gazed down, with a shocked expression on her face. A handful had come out in her fingers. The blood began to ooze again. Her dark eyes were wide in her dusty face.

'Your head's smashed up.' Jonathan said, feeling sick.

She managed another smile; her teeth and gums looked yellow against her grimy skin.

'It's OK. Scalp wounds always bleed a lot. I learned that at Red Cross.'

164

'What are we going to do?' Jonathan asked, tears welling again in his eyes.

'We'll just have to wait until they come.' The girl squeezed his hand tightly. 'It'll be all right, Jonathan. People always get rescued.'

Jonathan rubbed his nose with the back of his hand. 'No they don't.'

'Well . . . we're going to be, so don't worry. We'll just wait here and when we hear them coming, we'll shout. OK?'

'OK,' Jonathan sniffed.

'Does your leg hurt?' Amita asked.

'Only when I try to move. It feels numb . . . up here.' Jonathan rubbed his groin.

'Do you think it's broken?'

'I don't know.'

'If it wasn't trapped under that beam I could probably tell if it was. We did it at Red Cross. I could make a splint . . .'

Jonathan didn't answer. There didn't seem to be any point in talking about it. His leg was stuck and that was that.

'Were you doing your Christmas shopping?'

'We don't really have a proper Christmas,' Amita said. 'I was watching a lady do a cookery demonstration upstairs and I'd just come down to look at the toys . . . it's my sister's birthday soon.'

'Oh . . .' Jonathan couldn't really think what it would be like, not having a proper Christmas.

They lay in silence. Jonathan began to shiver. He felt sick again. It was that horrible smell . . .

'What's that smell, Amita?'

'I don't know.'

'It's horrible.'

'Yes.'

Jonathan's teeth were chattering. He felt a movement beside him. He opened his eyes to see Amita struggling to take off her tracksuit top. She put it over him, tucking it round his chin as if he was a baby. Then she lay close to him again. She put her arm across his chest. He could smell the faint aroma of perspiration. Of fear.

Warmer, he felt better.

The light from the window gradually faded. Soon it was pitch dark. Silent. Even the steady drip of the fractured water pipe had ceased. Jonathan thought about his mum, his dad. They'd come up to London for the day, Christmas shopping. Mum said she was glad to get away for a bit. Some men had been digging the road up outside their house for weeks and she was fed up with the mess.

'They've all gone home,' Jonathan whispered. 'They've given up looking.'

Amita shook her head. 'No, they won't do that.

I've seen it on television – when bombs go off and earthquakes and things. They always look for ages and ages.'

Jonathan didn't know how, but he must have fallen asleep. Wild nightmares haunted his brain. Once, he awoke, hearing a cry. Then he realized it was coming from him. Beside him, Amita hugged him close.

'It's OK, Jonathan, she murmured. 'They'll be here soon.'

He began to cry again. His throat was so dry he thought he was going to choke. A vision of a cool McDonald's vanilla milkshake floated before his eyes – a vision so clear he could almost feel the thick, creamy taste on his tongue. He felt ashamed. A big boy of eight – crying. His mum had always told him it was all right for boys to cry too – it wasn't only girls who were allowed. He felt ashamed all the same. Crying wouldn't do any good at all.

Jonathan awoke finally to a new orchestra of sound. Light was streaming through the shattered, jagged panes in the basement window. He could hear a faint, insistent tap–tapping above his head. There was a sharp ring of a hammer hitting metal and the deep, rhythmic hum of a compressor somewhere in the road.

He nudged Amita.

'Amita, wake up.'

The girl turned stiffly. She sat up, then groaned, putting her hand to her head.

Turning, she smiled. 'What . . .?'

'That noise . . .'

Amita cocked her head to one side. 'It's them,' she said. 'I knew they'd come.' She coughed, trying to clear her throat. Then she shouted, 'We're here! Help! We're here!'

But her shouting dislodged some of the plaster from the ceiling. It fell down like pink, choking snow. Then a big lump fell, striking her on the shoulder. Jonathan clutched her arm.

'Don't,' he hissed. 'Don't.' Jonathan could hardly bear to look. Supposing that other beam fell down on top of them; supposing that cracked wall caved in . . .

They waited . . . And waited . . . After a while, the tapping stopped.

'They've gone,' Jonathan whispered, his voice trembling. 'They've gone.'

Amita took hold of his arms. 'Jonathan, you've got to be brave!'

'I'm trying,' he sobbed.

'And you're doing very well. I've got a little brother about your age. He wouldn't be nearly as brave as you're being . . . but you mustn't give up. OK?'

169

Jonathan wiped his nose with the back of his hand. 'OK.'

Amita began to talk to him then. She told him about her house and her brothers and sisters. About her father who owned a shop and her mother who helped out, serving people from behind the counter. She told him about her grandmother and grandfather who had come from a place called Uganda when there was a war. They'd had to hide from a cruel dictator who was killing everyone. They had come to live in England so their children could grow up safely. They had been *really* brave, she told him. They'd arrived with nothing but the clothes they stood up in.

'Tell me about your family, Jonathan.'

'There's me and my mum and dad,' Jonathan told her.

'What do they do?'

'My mum works at home. She sews curtains and things.'

'What about your dad?'

'He works in an office and . . .' Jonathan brightened up a bit. 'He's a football referee too . . . do you like football?'

Amita grinned. 'Yes, it's great.'

Jonathan was beginning to feel tired again. All he wanted to do was go to sleep. His leg was beginning to hurt again, too. He must have moved in the night and twisted it. He closed his eyes.

Amita nudged him. 'Hey, Jonathan, you'd better not go to sleep.'

'Why not,' he mumbled.

'In case the rescuers come back.'

'I don't care.'

'Jonathan . . . Jonathan . . .'

From way above there came a rumble, then the sound of falling masonry. There was the noise of a hammer again and a machine of some kind. It sounded like one of those big diggers used on building sites.

'Jonny, Jonny, they've come back. They've got a machine. Listen . . .'

As Amita spoke, a large beam above their heads moved to one side. Electricity cables snapped, sparking like fireworks.

Jonathan struggled to sit up. 'No . . . no, they mustn't move anything else, they mustn't!'

Amita looked up fearfully. 'It's all right, it's stuck against that pillar. I don't think it's going to fall . . .'

'No,' Jonathan cried. 'It's the sparks.'

'It's OK, they're not near enough to hurt us.'

'Amita, don't you see . . .' Jonathan said urgently. 'It's that smell. I've remembered what it is. It's gas.'

'Gas!'

'Yes, they've been digging up the road outside our house to lay pipes. There was a leak or something. It smelt just like that!'

'Oh, no!' Amita looked up at the naked, dangling wire, still sparking. She wiped the back of her hand across her brow. Jonathan could see she was sweating – fear like crystals in the palm of her hand.

A lump of masonry fell with a crash. Rubble scattered. The girder imprisoning Jonathan's leg moved slightly. He screamed and covered his head with his arms.

'No! Stop!' Amita shouted, looking up again, panic-stricken. 'Stop . . . you'll kill us. Please!'

Somewhere above, the machine rumbled on . . . and on . . .

After a minute, Amita spoke again.

'Jon! Jon!'

Jonathan looked at her.

'Jon, we've got to let them know we're here. Make them stop digging.'

Jonathan shook his head. 'How? They haven't heard us shouting, they're making too much noise.'

The smell was getting stronger now. As if the shifting beam had opened up the broken pipe more than ever.

Jonathan could see Amita sitting with her head in her hands. She fumbled in the pocket of her tracksuit trousers and gave him a hanky. 'Here,' she said, 'hold this over your nose.'

'No.' Jonathan put his hand into his own pocket. 'I've got one, you use yours.'

Out with his hanky tumbled the present he'd bought for his dad.

'Jonny . . .' Amita had tied the scarf round her face like cowboys did in those old Western movies Jonathan's dad liked.

He tried to do the same. As Amita helped him, she said, 'Jonny, see that gap over there?'

Jonathan turned his head. Across, by the exit, a gap had opened up in the ruined wall. 'Yes,' he said, his voice muffled by the handkerchief. He could still smell the gas, even through the material.

'I'm going to try to get over there.'

'I don't think you should. You'll knock something . . . or that cable might fall on top of you.'

'I've got to, Jonathan . . . before it's too late.'

'All right.' Jonathan lay back with a sigh. He didn't really care what Amita did. They were going to die in here and that was that. If they didn't get blown up or electrocuted, they'd be squashed to death by bricks and stuff. It was only a matter of time.

The girl shook him. 'Jonathan, wake up. I need you.'

'What for?'

'To warn me if anything starts moving again.'

'I can't.'

'Yes you can . . . Sit up. Now!'

Jonathan sat up.

Amita gave him a hug. He could smell the

dry, plaster-filled dust on her face and hair. She left him and began to crawl across the floor. Her body left a trail in the dirt and rubble. Jonathan saw her move a great piece of cracked concrete to one side. A pile of boxes trembled, then fell on top of her. She brushed them aside impatiently. In front of the newly opened gap, a doll's pram rested on its side, twisted and smashed almost beyond recognition. Jonathan thought again of the lady with the pram who had been standing beside him looking at the racing-car models. He'd seen her before, asking the assistant about the golf clubs. He remembered she had smiled at him and the baby had chuckled . . .

The severed head of a rocking horse lay near the broken pram.

When Amita reached the gap, she turned. She lifted her arm and waved.

'I made it, Jonny.'

'Yes,' he called.

'You OK?'

'Yes.' He didn't know if she heard him. His voice sounded so weak and peculiar it was as if it belonged to someone else. He wished like anything that he could have a drink of water.

'Help!' Amita put her head between two criss-cross fallen girders. She shouted through the gap. 'Help us! Please!'

She turned. Even through the gloom, Jonathan

174

could see desperation on her grimy face.

'It's no good,' she called. 'It's hopeless. We could be down here for days and they wouldn't ever know.'

Jonathan suddenly remembered something he'd seen on television. Pictures of people being found in the wreckage of buildings, not only days after they'd been buried, but weeks sometimes. The rescuers had got dogs, trained especially to sniff people out. Jonathan liked dogs. His dad had a dog when he was a boy, but Jonathan's mum said they made too much mess. 'He was great . . . Rusty, he was called,' Jonathan's dad had said. 'Ever so good. I trained him with a special . . .'

Jonathan's hand closed over the little box by his side.

'Amita,' he called urgently. 'Amita, come here!'

Amita crawled slowly back to him. She put her arm across his shoulders. She took the hanky from her face. The ruined basement seemed to echo with the thunder of the overhead machine. All around them dust and debris began falling. Then, suddenly, the machine stopped.

Jonathan saw tears in Amita's dark eyes. 'I'm sorry, Jonathan.'

Jonathan thrust the box into her hand. 'Look!' he said. 'Take this . . . my dad won't mind if it's been used. Quick, before they start that thing up again.'

Amita brushed her tears away impatiently. Then a slow grin spread across her face when she saw what Jonathan had given her.

Carefully, slowly, Amita crawled back to the gap. She tore open the box and lifted something to her lips. She took a deep breath. A shrill whistle rang out. The sound seemed to bounce round the basement, out through the gap and up towards the rescuers above.

Jonathan wrenched off the handkerchief. If Amita could be brave, then so could he. Eyeing the sparking cable warily, he lifted his chin and took a deep breath. 'HELP!' he shouted. 'HELP!'

Amita blew the whistle again and again and again.

Then the machine rumbled into movement once more.

Jonathan saw Amita fall to her knees, her head in her hands.

It seemed a million years before anything else happened. First, the sound of a faraway bark, then a small scrabbling sound. Then, suddenly, like the sun coming out, a light shone through the gap. A moving light. Then a flash of colour. It looked like a yellow helmet, but Jonathan couldn't be sure. He saw Amita look up and stretch out her arm. The light shone on her face and he saw tears streaming from her eyes.

A hand came through the gap and reached for her.

'You all right, love?' a deep voice boomed.

'Please tell them to stop digging,' Amita shouted desperately. 'The gas pipe's broken and the electricity cables are sparking. Everything's moving . . . Tell them they've got to stop!'

Jonathan heard a shout, then another further away. Then there was silence. All Jonathan could hear was the sound of his own breath coming out in a huge sigh of relief. He saw Amita turn and point in his direction. 'And there's a little boy . . .'

'It's all right, love,' the voice said. 'We'll have you both out in no time.'

Then there was a loud rumble and stuff began falling. Jonathan heard Amita scream, then the whole world disappeared in a rain of dust.

Jonathan awoke to cold air on his face. He opened his eyes. He moved. One leg. The other was encased in some kind of stiff board. The now-familiar pain shot up to his groin. Something was attached to a needle going into his arm. He was lying on a stretcher with someone bending over him. His mum. Tears were streaming down her face and falling on to the red blanket that covered him. His dad stood beside her, his new referee's whistle dangling on a string from his hand. His other hand held Jonathan's so tightly it almost hurt. People milled around, talking. Some were laughing. There were two men in orange waistcoats holding collie dogs on leads. One of the dogs was barking.

Jonathan tried to sit up.

'Where's Amita?' He looked around in panic. There were a load of people standing behind barriers, watching. Anxious-looking people. Some crying. A line of ambulances with their blue, flashing lights, waited . . .

'I'm here.'

Jonathan turned in the direction of the voice. The white bandage round Amita's head looked like a turban. She sat on the kerb. A lady in a sari stood behind her, hugging a tall man with a dark beard.

'There you are, Jonny.' Amita smiled. 'I told you they'd come.'

A GAP IN THE DARK

by Helen Dunmore

'Com-ing!'

'She never counts up to twenty!' hissed Matthew as we skidded across the polished hall. No-one was around to stop us, so up the stairs we went, three at a time, never mind the noise.

Anne was slow. She'd still be in the kitchen asking Eliza, 'Did you see them? Which way did they go? You've *got* to tell me!'

We raced along the gallery, and nearly cannoned into Mistress Bowman, who was carrying a heap of linen from one of the bedrooms. I slowed down and curtsied politely, but she frowned and said, 'Not so fast, Judith. Matthew, surely you should be at your studies.' She looked at me coldly. Perhaps she thought I was stopping Matthew from working

at his Latin? No, it was more than that. She'd
changed. She never smiled at me any more, or
asked after my parents. Perhaps she didn't like me
coming to the Hall? But I hadn't got time to think
about that.

'In here,' said Matthew, and pushed me into a
small bare room. I'd never been there before. It
was square, with panelled walls, and there was no
furniture but a little white bed in the corner, and
a candlestick on the floor beside it. The room was
right at the end of the passage, and if Anne came
we weren't going to get away. I looked out of the
window but it was much too high for us to climb
down over the roof. And there was Anne again.

'I'm com–ing. I know where you are!'

She didn't, of course. She always said that.
She was still down in the hall, from the sound
of it. But what was Matthew doing, feeling along
the panels, pressing, stopping, pressing again? His
hands looked like Blind Thomas's when he tapped
his way through our village. A dark gap appeared
where the wall had been. A hole. What was it?
Matthew shoved me forward.

'Quick! Get in!'

I stepped over the threshold and into the hole.
I couldn't see much and I held my hands out,
feeling for the wall. There was nothing but cool,
empty, black space. Matthew bent down and pulled
something. Very smoothly and quickly the door

slid shut. Black, velvety darkness covered me like a mask. I raised my hands to my face as if to pull it off. I couldn't see my fingers. I couldn't see anything. I took a step back but the floor seemed to swing under me and I was afraid I'd fall.

Matthew whispered, 'There. She'll never find us now.'

He was so near, I could feel his warmth. It wasn't so bad with both of us there, close together, but I'd have hated to be shut in there on my own. The darkness was stifling – not like night-dark or any dark I've ever known. I strained my eyes and red blobs floated in front of them.

'Where are we?' I whispered.

'Ssh, she's coming.'

We heard Anne. First of all, the door banged open and there was a triumphant shout of 'Got you!' which tailed off into, 'Judith? Matthew? I know you're in here. You're only teasing me. I shall tell Mother.' She moved round the room. She must have been just the other side of the panelling, so close we could have touched her but for the wood in our way. Everything went silent, but I felt she was still there, perhaps listening for us. Then, very slowly and disappointedly, her feet went away.

'She's gone.'

'I wish we had a candle.'

'There's nothing much to see. Just a cell, then

181

the passage goes right back.'

'How strange. You wouldn't expect to find anything like this in a new building.'

Bowman Hall had been built fifteen years ago, by Matthew's father. It was the finest house for miles around.

'My father had the hole put in,' said Matthew. 'It was done on purpose.'

'Why?'

'In case anyone ever needed to hide. No-one knows about it. Only my mother and father, and me, and you. And perhaps Eliza does.'

'And the builders.'

'No. Only one man worked on the hole. My father trusted him.'

I didn't like talking without being able to see Matthew's face. We found ourselves whispering, even though we knew Anne had gone. The darkness pressed down on me, making me feel tired.

'Let's go out. I'm sure she's gone.'

Matthew moved and I heard a tiny click, the sort a well-oiled lock makes. Then a slice of white appeared, like a slice of cake. It hurt my eyes. We stumbled out of the hole, blinking, and Matthew quickly closed up the panel again. You couldn't see a trace of the door once it was shut, no matter how closely you looked. Then we heard Mistress Bowman's voice calling, 'Matthew! Matthew!'

She sounded angry. Anne must have said we'd

tricked her and run away. We often did. It was Anne who wanted to play hide-and-seek, not us.

'I must go home,' I said quickly, before anyone else could suggest it.

'Judith. You won't tell anyone about it, will you? It's very important.'

'Course I won't. I've never told on you, have I?'

I saw suddenly how important it was to Matthew. He looked older, and serious.

'Listen,' I said, 'I'm your friend. Of course I'll keep it secret.'

'Because one day . . . we might need to use it.'

That was the last time I was asked to visit Matthew at the Hall. After that everything changed. We had to meet down by the river, or in the woods, where no-one saw us. My mother kept me busy milking and churning with my sister Becky. When I said I wanted to see Matthew, she frowned, the way Mistress Bowman had done.

'You're to keep away from the Bowmans now, Judith. These are dangerous times for friendships between them and us. Don't you know they follow the old religion? You know what that means?'

I nodded. I did know. I'd heard it all round the village. Papists were dangerous. They wanted to kill our Queen and bring the King of Spain here to rule over us. There were plots everywhere. We'd have good men burnt alive at Smithfield again, the way it was under Bloody Mary. Ours was a good Protestant village, loyal to the Queen. That was what they said, but I knew it couldn't all be true. After all, Matthew was my friend. And I noticed that my mother and father never joined in when such things were said. I looked at my mother. Her face was anxious. Afraid. Afraid for me, the way she used to be when I played too near the fire when I was little.

'You must tell Matthew you have work to do at home. It's true enough.'

'The Bowmans are our neighbours, Susannah,' said my father.

'Don't let anyone hear you talking like that, John. Don't you know that there are Government spies everywhere, even in our village?'

A look passed between my parents. A look I couldn't understand. There was a secret, and I was shut out of it.

Suddenly it seemed as if everyone in our village was whispering about the Bowmans. People said a woman had been executed in York for hiding a Papist priest. Margaret something, her name was. Everyone was afraid. It's hard to describe what it was like. The whispering was like a shadow which covered everything and got in everywhere. What if the Bowmans were plotting? What if they were hiding priests? Would they bring down the Government spies and torturers on us all? My mother

184

listened, but I noticed that she never said a word. She didn't smile any more, either, and there was a new line on her forehead, between her eyes.

I was taking a basket of eggs down the village street when I first saw the man. He was on a fine mare, but she was worn out and sweating, with a white lather on her flanks. He was a gallant in a feathered hat and a velvet cloak, but he was covered in dust and dirt as if he'd come a long way, riding hard. He slowed the mare beside me and I could smell the heat of her. She was trembling and her flanks were going in and out, quickly. I knew she could not go on more than a mile.

'Is there a tavern here where I can rest myself and the mare?' he called.

'Joe Barraclough will serve you, sir. You'll find him outside the tavern.'

Joe was always outside the tavern, lounging and drinking ale in the sun while his wife cooked and served and wiped and cleaned. Still, he'd feed and groom the mare. He was good with horses.

'Thank you,' said the man. He smiled at me, and I noticed how warm his smile was – not at all like the gallants in York who'd as soon ride their horses' hooves over your feet as slow down for you. Then, suddenly, his smile froze. He stared at me. His eyes widened, almost as if he recognized me – as if he was about to say my name.

185

'Who are you?' he asked, in a small dry voice. His throat must have been full of dust.

'My name is Judith, sir. Judith Hestone.'

He let his breath out in a sigh. 'Ah. Hestone. Of course.' His hands were tight on the reins. The mare shivered, then put her head down and nuzzled my hand. I was burning with questions. Why '*of course*'? Why did he seem to know me?

'Joe Barraclough's tavern,' he said, as if remembering something a long way back. 'I must go there now. Goodbye, Judith,' and he walked the mare on, leaving me looking after him.

It was not so long after that I saw a knot of people coming up to our door. That wasn't unusual. People often came to talk to father about disputes and troubles, because he could usually calm them down and find an answer. I loitered round to listen.

'You know that fine gallant in the tavern . . .'

'I swear he's not what he seems . . .'

'Joe found a box in his saddle-bag . . .'

'Evil doings — he's got a prayer book with him full of Papish prayers . . .'

'And look at his face. And the way he limps. He's no gallant. He's a priest for sure, dressed up to fox us . . .'

'And where's he going, I should like to know?'

'Bowmans! Bowman Hall for sure!'

'Bowmans!'

They all took it up, their faces red and glistening. Father couldn't calm them this time. My mother stood beside him, her face white and frantic, arguing against the people. They wouldn't listen to her, either. I'd never seen her like that before. First they wanted to seize the man at once, and tie him in Joe Barraclough's stable till the Queen's men could get here. Then another said we ought to pretend nothing was amiss and let him go on up to Bowman Hall. We'd ride for the Queen's soldiers and they'd catch him up there and catch the Bowmans too, for sheltering a Papist priest. We'll do this, they said. No, we'll do that. I stood there, feeling cold, looking at faces. There was Simon Tolliver, who rented two fields from the Bowmans. He always said the rent was too high.

'We'll lead the soldiers to Bowmans!' he shouted.

We. I was in the crowd, part of it. But was I? Matthew was my friend, more than anyone else in the village. Matthew trusted me.

'Did I ever tell on you?' I'd said. I'd told him I could keep a secret. I was his friend. I didn't have to do anything to betray Matthew. All I had to do was do nothing and stand there, part of the crowd. My friend. Matthew. I saw his face in front of me, the way it was once, white and sick because he'd hit a trout's head on a stone to kill it and it wouldn't stop

187

flapping. I'd taken the slippery thing from him and struck it on the stone again. I never minded things like that.

I slipped back slowly out of the crowd so no-one would see me go. My heart was banging. They would capture the Bowmans, Matthew and Anne and all his family. And what would they do to them? I'd heard of people being questioned, put on the rack to make them talk. Better not think about it. I went round the back of our house, keeping close to the hedge, then through the gate into the pastures. This way I could go across country to Bowman Hall. It wasn't more than a mile from the village, and I could run. I could run Becky to a standstill any day, and even Matthew couldn't beat me. They would let the priest go off on horseback, round by the lane, thinking that no-one suspected him. I would cut across and be able to warn him before he reached the house. How long would it take to fetch the Queen's men? Not long. There were soldiers quartered at Riddal.

I'm a good runner, but every breath burned and my legs were shaking as I reached the top of the lane and flopped down on the verge. I couldn't hear anything. Had he passed already? No. There it was, the faint picking noise of hooves. In a few minutes he came round the corner of the lane, going slower than ever. He was urging the mare on.

'Come on, good girl Bess . . .'

I stood up slowly so as not to frighten the mare or the man. He knew me, and stopped, looking surprised.

'You're wandering far from home, Judith.'

It might have been because I'd been running, but I couldn't speak properly. I panted.

'They're getting the Queen's men. They know who you are. I came to warn you.'

His eyes went wide and still. The mare trembled all over as if she felt something.

'How long will it take till they get here?'

'I don't know. Not more than an hour. They've only to go to Riddal, and they've taken horses.'

'I'll have to leave the mare. Go across country . . .' He was thinking aloud.

'No!' I said. 'You'll be caught. You can't hide in those clothes.'

Then I remembered the hole, and what Matthew had said.

'*One day we might need to use it.*'

One day was now. I mustn't tell the priest about it yet, in case we were caught before we got to the Hall. He might give away the Bowmans' secret, if they tortured him. People did.

'There's a place. A hiding-place up at the Hall.'

Then he asked me a question I didn't understand then. 'Did your mother send you?'

190

'No, she doesn't know anything about it. Quick, we've got to hurry!'

'I'll leave the mare here,' he said. 'Better if they think I've taken to the woods. Poor old girl, poor Bess, will you fend for yourself?'

'She's a fine mare. Someone'll take her, and be glad to do it,' I said.

He slid off the saddle and stood wearily in the lane. I could see how stiff his legs were. The mare put her head down and began to graze. He undid his saddle-bag and slung it on his back. It looked strange on top of his rich cloak. He walked so slowly, limping.

'Quick!' I said. 'Men from the village will come up to guard the lanes while others fetch the soldiers.'

He hobbled along, not at all like a fine gentleman.

'Can't you go faster?' I begged.

He laughed quietly, as if it didn't matter at all.

'I had a taste of the rack once,' he said. 'They let me go that time, but it's left a mark on my bones.'

And yet he was still going round the country, dodging and hiding, even though he knew what would happen if they caught him.

'You could take my arm,' I said.

We went as fast as we could, him hobbling and leaning on me. My shoulder ached from his

191

weight. If only he'd left the saddle-bag we'd have got on better, but when I suggested he hide it in a ditch, he gasped.

'No. That's why I'm here.' I knew then that he must have his priestly things in the bag, and I didn't complain about it any more.

The Hall was very quiet. We came in the back way, through the stableyard, with the doves bubbling and cooing, and Matthew's mare, Star, looking over her stable-door at us. I pushed open the kitchen door and there was Eliza. She was stirring milk over the fire, and she turned and saw us.

'What's this, Judith? You know you're not supposed to come here—'

'Quick. He's a priest. The Queen's men are coming. The men from the village are fetching them. They want to trap the Bowmans.'

'God have mercy on us, and Mistress Bowman's sick with an ague. I was making this posset for her. And the master's away.' Eliza held out the mixture of milk and honey as if it would solve everything.

'Where's Matthew?' I said. At least he'd help me do something. Then Eliza changed. Her big body became purposeful. Calling for Matthew, she steered us through the kitchen. A door upstairs opened and I heard Matthew clattering down.

'Where's Anne?' I asked. 'She mustn't see us.'

'Now where's Miss Anne? Ah, she's in the

orchard, picking up eggs. The hens are laying astray again.'

Possets, hens, eggs. Was that all Eliza could think of?

'Matthew!'

It didn't take more than a minute to explain to Matthew. It was strange. It seemed as if he was prepared for this. Almost as if he'd been waiting for it.

'He was going to go off cross-country but I brought him here because of the secret place,' I said, and Matthew nodded. His freckles stood out, the way they did when he was angry. He bowed to the priest.

'Father,' he said, 'you are very welcome here. We'll have to get him upstairs, Judith.'

Together, we helped the priest up the stairs. He could have managed it, only we had to hurry. At the top I looked back and saw the dusty treads we'd left across Eliza's polished floor.

'Eliza! Wipe off all the marks. They'll see where we've gone.'

We looked out of the low passage window, where the window-seat was. Matthew and I used to sit there on rainy days, telling stories and eating Eliza's honeycakes. There was the orchard. There was Anne in her blue dress, bending down and searching the long grass for eggs. And there, beyond Anne . . . Two heads. At the orchard wall. They bobbed, then looked up and over. We sank out of sight, but I'd recognized them.

'Sammy Orr and Ben Striddle.'

'What about Anne? They'll frighten her.'

'She doesn't know anything and anyone can tell that she doesn't. You can't call her in now.'

We were in the little square room again. It was hot with the sun pouring into it. The priest let go of our shoulders and straightened himself. Matthew was already feeling the panels, trying to find the catch. His hands were clumsy but at last the panel slid and darkness appeared. The priest raised his hand. I didn't know what he was doing at first, then he made the sign of the cross. He was blessing us.

'Food!' I said. 'Have we got time?'

'They're watching the house. And Anne might come in and see me carrying it up. We haven't got time.'

No food or drink then. Just darkness. The priest stepped carefully over the threshold.

'Pass me my bag,' he said. 'Gently . . . What's in that bag is more important than I am.'

'Matthew,' I said, 'I'll have to go in with him.'

He frowned. I could almost see his thinking pass over his face.

'But it might be days, Judith. When the Queen's men get here they'll search the house but they won't leave straightaway. If they suspect there's a

194

priest-hole they'll camp here and try to starve him out.'

'I can't leave now. They'll see me. They'll know I've come from the village to warn you. They know I'm your friend. They might burn the house down . . .'

It had been done to other houses. We both knew it.

'I'll bring you food. I swear it. Three scratches on the door and it'll be me. There's water in a pitcher just inside the panel, on your left.'

'But why? I mean, how did you know?'

'It's always there. Just in case . . .'

Just in case. We looked at each other, then I stepped forward and the panel slid shut behind me. Darkness moved all over me like velvet, like something alive. I could hear the priest's breathing, harsh and laboured, close to me.

'Move back,' I said. 'The passage goes back.'

We edged back, back, back, until we struck cold stone wall. There was a dank smell, as if the air had been here for a long time, never changing or blowing away. It made me shiver. He must have felt it because he said in the same murmur which you couldn't have heard more than three feet away: 'Don't be afraid.'

Don't be afraid! He was the one who ought to be afraid. Or perhaps I was, too. After all, I was hiding a priest. Betraying the people of my own village. Helping a priest to safety. That's what they'd say.

'*How could you do it, Judith?*'

Bloody Mary. Bonfires at Smithfield. Bringing back the Papists. The King of Spain ruling over England. But it wasn't like that. Matthew was a Papist, and I was a Protestant, but we were friends. That felt more important than anything. And I could tell from his breathing that the priest was in pain. And what would they have done to him if they'd caught him?

We waited. My breathing was jerky and my heart banged until I couldn't tell if I was hearing footsteps or not. Then, at last, we felt them. The crash of heavy boots vibrating through the house, shaking the floor, coming closer and closer. I'd never heard footsteps like those in any house before; footsteps which didn't care what noise they made, what damage they did. The air seemed to shake with them. Thick, dark, shaking air pressed against my face, filling my ears and my eyes and my mouth. Voices shouted – loud outdoor voices – angry, echoing from room to room. They didn't belong in this house. Then a crash, and a cry, and another crash as if something had been flung against the panelling. Or someone. They were in the room, just the other side of the wooden wall. I was shaking – or was it the priest shaking? Was it my hand slippery with sweat, or his? I didn't care. It didn't matter.

Then the batter of noise stopped. Everything was quiet as the inside of a grave. I knew they were listening. Listening for us. Waiting for us to give ourselves away by a cough or a whisper. Then more shouting, more footsteps, but going away from us now. I followed them in my mind – across the room, through the door, down the polished gallery.

A murmur in my ear. The priest.

'Don't stir. It's a trick. To make us think they've gone.'

I couldn't stand up any longer. I slid down to the floor and crouched there. I tried to shut my mind but I kept hearing things, remembering things:

'. . . *that woman executed in York . . . Margaret something . . . two priests hanged at Tyburn, they say . . . took them in for questioning . . . put them on the rack . . . they soon talked . . .*'

They would torture the priest to make him talk. Would they torture me? If they asked me questions, would I be able to stop myself answering them? We crouched in the dark, side by side, peering into nothing.

'You're a brave girl,' the priest whispered. Then he added in a low voice, so low I was hardly sure if I'd heard it or not, 'Like your mother.'

'Like Mother? What do you mean? Do you know Mother?'

'You're old enough to keep a secret, Judith?'

Here we were, hiding in the dark from the Queen's men who might kill us if they found us, and he was asking me if I was old enough to keep a secret. He must have realized how stupid it was, because he said, 'I'm sorry. Of course you are. Yes, I knew your mother long ago, when we were children. That's how I knew who you were – you're very like her. Then we grew up and she married your father and came here, and I went abroad.'

'She never told me anything about you.'

'Perhaps she thought it was best not.'

My mother seemed like a different person suddenly. She'd had friends I'd never even known she had. And they grew up together; he must have been important to her. But he became a priest. I had so many questions to ask—

Three scratches, and then the white gap in the dark. It hurt my eyes again. Matthew's voice.

'Quick. Over here.'

We stumbled towards the light. It was Matthew. He pushed past me and shoved a basket and a bundle into the hole, then hauled me out. The priest let go of my hand. I looked back, but he didn't move. I could see his quiet face in the light from the panel door before Matthew shut it again and left him there alone.

'Hurry. We can get you out. All the women and children from the village are up here, round the house. They came with the soldiers. They're making sure no-one escapes. Go straight down the stairs and into the kitchen. There's a guard on the main door, but if anyone sees you, say you pushed your way in. If you curse us and yell enough they'll believe you. Once you're in the stableyard you can slip into the crowd and start shouting like the rest of them. Everyone knows you.'

'I shan't do that. I shan't yell and shout like them,' I said angrily.

'You will. You've got to. Then no-one'll guess.'

And I did. I cursed the Bowmans for Papists, I shook my fist and spat and swayed and yelled with the crowd. The soldiers wanted us there, but they didn't want us to get too rough. All the village was there, but my mother and father never came. When we surged forward, the soldiers pushed us back, showing their pikes. It wasn't till nightfall that some of the crowd began to get bored and drift back to the village. After all, there was nothing to see. Mistress Bowman sick with ague. And she'd been good to many in the village in her time. She'd made medicines out of herbs, and sent wine to people who were sick. People began to remember it. They grew cold and shifted their feet and thought of home.

But I stayed. I stayed and watched it all. Three soldiers skewered live hens on their swords: Mistress Bowman's hens, whose eggs Anne had been hunting. Others lit a fire in the stableyard while James the stable-boy looked on, not daring to protest, white with fear that the stables would catch fire and the horses burn alive. The officers watched and smiled.

My mother ran out to meet me as I came in through our gate. Her face was pale.

'Where have you been, Judith?'

'Up at the Hall.'

She reached out and hugged me so tight I could hear her heart bumping.

'They haven't caught him,' she whispered.

'No. He's hidden. Mother—' But I didn't go on. She hadn't told me, and it was her secret.

'All the village is up there,' I said. 'I hate them!'

'You mustn't do that,' said my mother. 'They are our neighbours. We have to live with them.'

They didn't find the priest that time. He crouched behind the panelling for three days while the soldiers sat in the kitchen and ate the hams and cheeses Eliza had put away for the winter, and drank all Mistress Bowman's mead and apple wine. At night they got drunk and roared out songs, keeping time with their fists and their boots. You could hear them all through the yards and the orchard and way down nearly to the village. From there people could see the fires they lit, leaping and roaring into the sky as if the Hall itself was on fire. But they didn't fire the Hall, not this time. They smashed Mistress Bowman's fine chair, and ripped her mattresses with their swords till the house was full of feathers, saying they were looking for the priest. They burned the henhouses and when they left they took Star with them, and they would have taken Matthew's father's mare if she hadn't been lame. I thought of how Matthew couldn't bear to knock the head of a trout against a stone, but he had to live for three days in that house with the soldiers listening for every sound, and his mother sick, and Anne whimpering with terror every time a soldier came into the room. It would keep on happening, over and over, I knew, as long as the Bowmans stayed Papist.

I saw the soldiers go. They had their packs clutched to them, full of what was left of the Bowmans' stores. And china, and glass, and everything they could carry. No matter if it smashed on the journey. I stood in the yard and watched the stragglers go. There were only a few of us from the village left now, and we didn't look at each other much. It was as if we were ashamed. I listened to their boots, going off down the lane, and stood there, watching the house. The sun was warm and the doves which were still alive were purring up on the roof. Soon the last few watchers would go back to the village, and I would knock softly on the side-door, and Matthew would let me in.

I had scarcely been home those past three days, except to eat and to sleep, but my mother knew where I was and she didn't stop me. She understood that I wanted to be where Matthew was, even if I couldn't help him. Once or twice she started to say something and I thought she was going to tell me about the boy she had known all those years ago, who was a Papist too. But it wasn't the right time. She kept her secret and I kept mine, but I knew one day we'd tell one another. The village people would say I'd betrayed them if they knew how I'd run across the fields to warn the priest and help him hide, but I knew now that my parents would be glad I'd done it. I'd kept Matthew's secret, and I could keep my mother's. I was part of it now.